Summer Shot

Wyverns Hockey Book Two

A.C. Wonderland

For the people who showed me my first five star romance story and who taught me what true unconditional love looks like - my parents. Your love story will always be one of my favorites. It's the reason I am obsessed with love.

Love you so much mom and dad (if you love me back. . . then please don't read chapter six or eighteen).

Summer Shot

Wyverns Hockey Book Two

A.C. Wonderland

Playlist

Scan the code below to listen to
the *Summer Shot* playlist on Spotify

Chapter One
I'll Be Fine – Meghan Moroney

Chapters Two and Three
Feels Like Summer – Samuel Jack

Chapter Four
Summertime – Kenny Chesney

Chapter Five
Summer Nights – Rascal Flatts

Chapter Six
You, Honey – Tucker Wetmore
Summer On Your Lips – Conner Smith

Chapter Nine
Boys Back Home – Dylan Marlowe and Dylan Scott

Chapter Twelve
Slow Down Summer – Thomas Rhett

Chapter Thirteen
The Girls – Meghan Moroney

Chapter Seventeen
There Goes That – Dylan Marlowe

Chapter Nineteen
Secrets – One Republic

Chapter Twenty-Three
Dirty Little Secret – All American Rejects

Chapter Twenty-Nine
Put it On Ice (Feat Hardy) – Thomas Rhett

Chapter Thirty-One
What I Want – Morgan Wallen and Tate McRae

Chapter Thirty-Two
Lucky – Meghan Moroney

Chapter Thirty-Four
He Loves You Not – Dream

Recap

Life-changing is the best way I can describe how the West Michigan Wyverns hockey team has impacted my life. Life altering in so many positive ways. My best friend and brother, Nick, and my dad, Nico, both were captains of the team over their hockey careers. Nick's time on the Wyverns ended quicker than anyone anticipated due to a tragic accident.

Anytime I think about that day, my body goes numb. Visions of the accident still haunt me. Somehow, I survived but I didn't feel like I was really living. The accident turned my life upside down.

Nick and I had big dreams and aspirations—together—with Nick as captain of the team his senior year, for the second year in a row, and me finally at West with him working on the Marketing and PR team supporting the Wyverns. But with the accident, that dream slipped out of reach.

Little did I know, he applied to the PR and marketing program on my behalf prior to the accident.

Deciding to come to WMU for the program was one of the hardest things I've ever done—the memory of my brother was everywhere—but it was also one of the most rewarding. I started to live my life again by forcing myself to be around hockey, a sport I have loved my entire life.

My dream career working in marketing for an NHL team started to feel like a possibility again with each day I focused on the Wyverns. I even had multiple articles published in USA Hockey Magazine—along with a lot of my hobby photography!

The game wasn't the only positive impact on me—the team on and off the ice really changed my heart. Bren, my best friend and cousin, led the PR team last year. I moved in with her and ate way too much bacon for breakfast. I was reunited with my childhood friend, Tyler Barret, who played hockey alongside my brother growing up and was like family to me.

Somehow, against all odds and against my own promise to myself that I wouldn't date, love found me in the form of the captain of the team, Lucas Donato. I was set on swearing off love because of trauma with my ex-boyfriend, but my heart couldn't ignore my feelings for Lucas. Lucas is great for me in every way humanly possible. I was, and still am, very smitten.

For the first time since sharing my secret with Nick, I started to open up about my abusive past relationship. Healing that was way overdue started to happen.

Tears were in full force last season when my brother's Wyverns jersey #88 was retired. The entire team, support staff, and marketing team wore special edition Nick Bellinger jerseys. Presales for them were massive, and so many people in the stands wore them too. The coolest part of the special edition jersey: Nick actually designed them himself. After finding his sketches in an old notebook, I knew that I wanted to honor him in a big way with his very own jersey.

My heart practically leaped out of my chest at the ceremony when my stepdad announced that he was starting the Nick Bellinger Foundation. My friends and stepdad somehow kept the foundation a secret from my mom and me. My eyes still brim with tears anytime I think about that heartfelt surprise.

The foundation supports grants and scholarships for youth hockey programs as well as providing college scholarship opportunities. All the money the marketing and PR team raised last season went to support the foundation.

But that's not all, the Wyverns would partner with the foundation as the main charity for seasons to come.

Last season had a lot of ups and downs. It had a lot of trial and trauma—for myself and the hockey team. The Wyverns became conference champions, having had one of the best regular season records in franchise history. Lucas and the Wyverns made it all the way to the Frozen Four, but they lost and didn't make it to the last round of the playoffs. Even still, it was an incredible season to be a part of.

I am really looking forward to the summer at West and a new season with less stress and heartache than the previous one.

Chapter One

Laur

The warm August sun shines bright on campus in Frostburg, Michigan. Somehow the summer flew by. In a few weeks, the West Michigan Wyverns hockey team will start their normal practice schedule. Meanwhile, my palms are perpetually sweating with anxiety as I prepare to lead the Wyverns' Student Marketing and PR Program for my senior year.

Out of the kindness of her heart, Bren, my cousin, best friend, and previous leader of the program, helped Libby and me conduct interviews over the summer before her sad departure. Bren literally bounced with joy when she received the opportunity to work in the PR department for the Red Wings NHL team a few months ago. She barged into my room and jumped on my bed, waking me up way too early. I'm just glad she left me with my new best friend Libby I met here at West last year.

Last season was unforgettable. The Wyverns made it all the way to the Frozen Four. Even though they didn't make it to the championship game, the team was H-O-T, *hot*. Not to toot my own horn, but the marketing and PR team went above and beyond last season. We published articles in *USA Hockey Magazine*, ran contests for signed posters raising an insane amount of money for our new main charity—the Nick Bellinger Foundation—and sold custom jerseys and calendars, both of which SOLD OUT! The hockey team quickly became the most popular crew on campus.

My heart races with excitement. All the new members of my marketing and PR team are finally here. An enormous smile overtakes my face knowing I'll get to introduce some of the new members to the hockey team today!

We selected two new sophomores and one new junior to join the small but mighty team. The new members have a much more diverse background outside of hockey, which I think will work to our advantage. Libby and I both have family ties to the sport—we practically bleed hockey—so I think the diverse background will really work to our advantage with getting even more engagement outside of just the school.

One of the sophomore girls, Raven, doesn't have any big connection to hockey, but has a great social media background with fashion and fundraising. My heart practically leaps out of my chest when I reviewed her application, eager for someone with extensive fundraising experience to join our team. She even transferred from another school to take the opportunity!

The sounds of skates and pucks scraping against the ice fill the air as I lead the girls into the arena while the guys are practicing. They trail behind me like precious, innocent little ducklings. Coach spots me and signals to give the team five more minutes.

Warmth fills me as my eyes find Lucas Donato—the captain of the team and my hotshot sexy boyfriend—in the sea of players on the ice. No matter how many times I see Lucas play hockey, my heart flutters every time I see him in his element.

After a few drills, Coach blows the whistle for the team to circle up and pauses practice, letting us have our planned interruption. I swoon as Lucas Donato tells the team to listen up at the introductions and instructions from me. He gives me a wink as I open my mouth to start my spiel, but someone else speaks up first.

"Hi, Luc." Raven interrupts in a coy tone. Raven, the ironically-blonde sophomore transfer, stares bright-eyed at Lucas, a flirtatious smile curling her freshly glossed lips.

A knot forms in my stomach. I'm used to girls gawking at Lucas, but this is the last place I expected to witness it.

"Raven?" Lucas' beautiful golden-brown eyes fill with recognition and confusion. How does he know Raven? She called him Luc. It's clear they know each other well . . .

Nausea threatens to consume me, but I keep my cool as I introduce the new girls, including Raven, and give the hockey team a quick rundown of interviews we will be conducting over the next few weeks.

Before I turn to leave with the rest of the girls, Lucas grabs my arm and pulls me to him. Jaw clenched and nostrils flaring, he steams with frustration.

"Lauren, how the hell is my ex-girlfriend part of your PR and marketing team? And why the hell is she?"

My heart plummets into my stomach. Lucas only has one ex-girlfriend that I'm aware of. I don't know her name or age, but I do know she wanted him to give up hockey . . . they broke up his freshmen year because of it.

How did I not know that Raven Matthews, the new sophomore lead on *my* team, was his ex-girlfriend?

More importantly, how the hell am I going to get through this season with my boyfriend's ex-girlfriend not only working closely with me but being around him 24/7? I just started finally working through my own past relationship trauma . . .

Now, I have no hope that this season is going to be less stressful, less traumatic, or less dramatic than last season.

In fact, I have a feeling it's going to be the exact opposite. It seems like one of my precious ducklings isn't so innocent.

A Few Months Earlier

Chapter Two
Laur

Summer in West Michigan is going to be heavenly. Last summer, I was a depressed mess with the loss of my brother, confining myself to my parents' house in Morgan, Illinois. I've never spent the summer away from my hometown. Needless to say, I'm looking forward to a summer just actually doing something and being somewhere other than the middle of nowhere, where there's one stop light and the closest Target is a half hour away.

With preparing to take over as lead for the Wyverns Student Marketing and PR team, I know I have a lot of work ahead. My stomach twists and turns with nerves, knowing I'm about to take the reins. Bren was the best leader the team could have asked for. Luckily, she will be around long enough to help Libby and me review applications.

Both horrified and honored by the amount of printouts, Bren, Libby, and I sift through the piles of applications in the living room. The applications seem never ending. Luckily with three of us, we can divide and conquer—each of us taking a third of the applications and selecting our top twenty. From there, we'll collectively agree on twenty to interview.

"How many more do you have left in your piles?" Libby groans, "We've spent so many hours already today."

Twenty out of five hundred didn't seem like much, until I remember the various rounds of interviews. The knot in my stomach sinks lower.

"It's only been about six hours, Lib," Bren says. "But we finally each have our top twenty candidates."

"It blows my mind that Laur never had to interview." Libby picks up another application packet.

"Yeah, mine too," I mutter back.

"You would have interviewed flawlessly anyways," Bren assures me.

Somehow Bren and my brother, Nick, circumvented that part when Nick applied on my behalf without my knowledge. It's the sweetest thing Nick ever did for me. I know he would be proud watching me run the program.

Hopefully, I won't run it to the ground.

Bren makes sure to remind me how ridiculous I am when I say "nonsense like that." She claims I'm the reason the program did so well last year, especially with launching a new special edition Nick Bellinger designed jersey and taking over as photographer for the team's annual sexy calendar shoot.

Good looks are *very* prevalent for the Wyverns hockey team, so they will always be easy to capture on and off the ice. But this year, there are going to be even better opportunities for interviews, articles and overall promotion of the team. The team is coming off a hot season last year and many seniors have high hopes for NHL opportunities.

"My interview *was* flawless. Right, Bren?" Libby doesn't wait for a reply. "Perfection, just like *the* Ryder King will be this year."

West has been blessed with freshman Ryder King—he's a godsend. He was the most in demand new player of the year. He turned down several top hockey schools, even Boston University and Michigan, to come play for West.

Everyone, even Lucas, boasts how lucky to have him we are, but it's rumored he's an insanely cocky playboy. I guess with a name like Ryder King, how could he not be? Maybe he'll give Blaine Mitchell a run for his money. As long as both boys don't cause drama with my team, their antics won't cause my heart rate to spike.

"We could pivot and talk about a strategy for the Elite Eight, if you are wanting a break, Laur," Bren suggests.

"Absolutely not." I throw a glare her way. "We need to finalize our team first before we dive into anything for next year."

After much debate with Libby and Bren, the Sexy Seven player focus is morphing into the Elite Eight. Plus, with Ryder being under a microscope I'm going to need an even larger support team this year with at least one social media guru. With the extra classes and certifications I've taken and much trial-and-error, I've become quite the expert myself. But Libby and most of the rest of the team from last year have really been more focused on the traditional PR side with press releases and article content.

"Has anyone found any candidates that have extensive social media experience?" I chew on the cap of my pen.

Bren shakes her head, while Libby just shrugs. *Very helpful, Lib.*

If none of the candidates that applied have extensive social experience, then the next best option is anyone who has run charity fundraisers. Raising money for the selected Wyverns' charities is the main goal of the PR and marketing program after, of course, highlighting and elevating the team. Promoting the team and events on social media will both be incredibly important—we want to spread the word and get people to the games and fundraiser events

I'm not trying to reinvent the wheel, but expanding the events where the hockey team is present will be a key focus this season, especially with Ryder King about to be a hot commodity on campus.

Bren suggests I take him on as my main focus. Not only is he going to be a crucial part of the team's image, but all eyes in the hockey world are going to be on him and wanting to know more about his season on the Wyverns.

The interview process flies by extremely fast despite being three full rounds. Anxiety fills me knowing the amount of work and hours that will go into the interview process. Thankfully a few months before last season was over, Bren and I started reviewing the top potential candidates who already applied before the deadline to ease into the process. Even though all the other leads in the six years of the program typically leave campus, Bren has claimed that starting her new job a few weeks later than planned will be both her goodbye and "welcome to the shit show" gift to me.

A knot forms in my stomach looking around the living room and taking in the chaos of applications scattered everywhere. My heart aches knowing Bren will leave soon, but I'm filled with a thrill knowing Libby's moving into Bren's old room, while Jaylin, our other house-mate, is going to be staying to finish her senior year.

"Can we *please* take a break?" Libby pleads, sprawling across the floor.

Bren's deep brown eyes lock with mine from the other side of the couch, waiting for my answer. We could all use it, but we need to narrow down to at least thirty applicants before the three of us head on a long summer weekend trip with some of the hockey team.

Daydreaming about Lucas shirtless on a beach, showing off his chiseled abs and alluring V that leads to my favorite body part of his has become a regular occurrence for me the last few days. I want more than anything to focus solely on his body intertwining with mine multiple times a day during this trip. But unfortunately, we needed to set up an interview days ago for that to happen.

"Sure, let's order dinner and grab some wine. At this rate, we are going to have to evaluate applications during our beach trip anyways," I let out an exaggerated breath, partly from exhaustion and partly from disappointment knowing we'll be working over the trip.

When Lucas agreed to go on a trip, his only stipulation was that he needed at least two hours a day to work out and an hour to himself. I knew there was no arguing with him about the workout—he was going to have to survive time away from the ice. I didn't ask what the hour to himself was supposed to be for; I just wanted to get away with my sexy boyfriend. There is no doubt in my mind Lucas will be forcing the guys to workout with him, so maybe the girls and I will be able to narrow down our piles of applications enough so we only need to sift through them during their workouts.

Reviewing applications doesn't sound like my ideal vacation, but at least I'll have a view of the beach. I already plan to convince Lucas a beach workout is the best option—the resistance from the sand will work their muscles harder. Plus, it'll be an even better view than just the beautiful beach.

"I'll make a deal with you," Libby says, pushing up onto her arm.

"About what? The applications?" I inquire.

"Yes," Libby responds. "We can open another bottle of wine, if we each go through the top five of each of our twenty candidates."

"Libby, I love you, but you don't have room to negotiate this," I laugh. "You're my second in command and unless we are bringing a non-experienced senior onboard, we need to re-review applications."

"No, no more!" Libby falls back on the sofa in defeat.

"I should be the one who can negotiate this shit. I don't even go to school here anymore!" Bren exclaims as she shuffles through papers.

Bren's not wrong, but I'm quick to remind her she's being paid a pretty nice stipend by the hockey team to stay onboard for two months.

"I'll make a deal with you both. We share our top three applicants. Then on our flights there, we review each other's piles and score everyone, including our own applicants with scores one through five. That way we can make a no pile and start to get interviews on the books."

"And more wine?" Libby perks up.

"On it!" Bren springs up off the couch and bolts to the kitchen to grab another bottle of red. Once we've all been topped off, Libby starts presenting her top three applicants.

A daze falls over me, I'm not fully listening to anything Libby says until she says something about a girl having a unique background in fundraising for fashion companies.

"No hockey ties?" I raise an eyebrow.

"None, but we have that part covered!" Libby hurries to add. "She has extensive experience working with large fashion brands on the fundraising and event planning side. I think she could bring a unique set of skills to the table and be a huge asset. She would come in as a sophomore transfer."

My eyes widen with intrigue. Libby knows I really want to focus on bigger, better fundraisers this year—a skillset like this could be just what we need to help support my vision. She has my full attention now.

"Tell me more."

Chapter Three
Lucas

Light streams through the windows in the living room where I sit and reminisce about last seasons, which feels like it just ended yesterday, but somehow it's May. I didn't take my team to the finals to win it all, but we made it pretty damn far getting to the Frozen Four. We persevered. We pushed ourselves harder than before. *And* we had some unnecessary obstacles like two of our key players getting benched for several games from a stupid, drunken night.

But that was nothing compared to finding out my girlfriend's abusive ex-boyfriend was on our biggest rival team. I ended up in the penalty box, but his face is still intact, which means I handled myself much better than I should have. Playing East Michigan while he's on the team will always infuriate me. With what Nathan Kovek did to Lauren . . . he should be in jail. Regardless of all the ups and downs, it's a season I will always be proud of—proud of myself as a player, proud of myself as a captain, and proud of myself as a man handling unnavigable situations.

Now, it's summer at West. Summer always takes more of a toll on me than I like to admit. Most people love the sun, the beach, time off and vacations. I was born to be on the ice as much as possible, which doesn't go hand in hand with any of those things.

Keith Hall, my roommate, best buddy and Wyvern's goalie, saunters into the living room from upstairs. I've got the TV and have been jumping from show to show, trying to find something to watch and relax.

"You excited to leave for the beach?" He asks blooping down next to me.

"I guess so." I shrug, pausing on the travel channel.

Somehow, Laur still convinced me to take a trip with plenty of sun and sand, but absolutely no ice rink. When she said *"It's our last shot at summer before being in the real world—it's our summer shot."* I couldn't argue. I'm not sure how I'm going to survive without ice time, but if anyone is worth it, it's her.

We agreed I would get at least three hours everyday for what I needed to do and the rest of the time to enjoy vacation. Two of those hours are designated for working out and forcing the rest of the team to join me. The other hour is just for myself to try to unwind without chaos around me.

"Why do you have such a hard time relaxing?" Keith asks.

I release my shoulders, not realizing they were tensed up.

"I've got a lot on my plate this season—" I flip through the channels"—you know that."

"Yeah, but the Wyverns are going to kick ass this season." Keith gets up to go to the kitchen, grabs himself a beer from the fridge, then sits at the table, scrolling through his phone.

I guess he's taking summer by the reins. Meanwhile, my stress level seems to rise daily, knowing I need to bring my suggestions on three players for alternative captains this year to Coach the day after we return from this trip. The team takes a vote and the coaching staff weighs in, but Coach Andres made it clear to me my recommendation will have the most weight on his final decision.

Keith is the most obvious choice. Despite his current 11:00 a.m. beer, Keith has always been a leader on the team. Not to mention he's one of the best goalies in college hockey.

Tyler Barret, one of our other close friends, is another option. Like me, Tyler lives and breathes the sport and will likely play for the NHL after our final season as Wyverns. Laur will deny this until her dying breath—but Tyler is a playboy.

In Laur's defense, he does hide it well. My number one focus right now is hockey and it should be the main priority for the entire team if we want to make it to the finals this year. Tyler might love hockey, but I think he'll put meeting girls and getting laid first on this trip. I'm curious to see how much he focuses on keeping up his workouts and helping me wrangle in the guys who complain about it.

Keith is another no brainer. If we didn't have such stellar seniors last year, I'm sure he would've already been an alternate captain. There are a few other seniors that could fit the bill, but I'm partial to adding a junior or even sophomore to the captain roster. If all the alternate captains are seniors, leadership will be gone after this year, which is the situation we're in now.

Last year, Liam Welsh and Conner Rizzo, were both alternate captains, while I was captain as a junior.

Liam has been my ride or die since I came to West my freshman year. It feels a little off without him around. Once the season starts, it's going to feel even weirder with the two of them gone. I still talk to them both every now and again, but they are super busy being big shots in the national hockey league—Liam playing for the Seattle Kraken and Conner for the New York Rangers. I'm insanely happy and proud of them both, but it doesn't make me wish they were here any less.

The junior candidates for alternate captain are plentiful. Blaine Mitchell might be a contender, but I'm not hopeful that he'll step up. He used to be the biggest problem child on the team, but he did turn things around at the end of last season.

For some reason, Blaine is coming on the beach trip with us. Last year, none of my friends would have wanted to be around him. So far this summer, he hasn't gotten in any brawls or tried to convince anyone else to get in any. Granted it's only been a few weeks of summer, but it's progress over his delinquent antics from last year. The trip will give me a better idea on how Blaine and Tyler are as leaders outside of the typical campus environment.

That leaves Ryder King, the godsend golden boy coming to West as a freshman, as my final contender. Every major college team chased him last year to recruit the kid. Rumor is he's better than Nick Bellinger, better than me, and the next Sidney Crosby.

We'll see about that.

I met him briefly when he came to watch us play a few games—he seemed like a normal, eager player to me, but there are countless rumors about him being demanding, selfish, and cocky as hell.

There have never been any freshmen in Wyverns history to be alternative captains. Even if he's a prodigy, I'm hesitant to make a freshman alternate captain when other players have put their blood, sweat, and tears into the team for countless hours over the years.

"Hey, when is Ryder King coming to campus?" Keith calls from the kitchen, snapping me out of my thoughts.

"Tomorrow," I respond. "But he still hasn't said if he is coming to the beach with us."

He's the only new player who was invited to join. Sure, he doesn't know any of us, but it would be a good opportunity for him to connect with the team off the ice. If I were him, I would be going, even if only to start making connections with my new teammates.

"I bet he'll join." Keith flops back down on the couch.

"If I were him, I'd be wanting to get to know the upperclassmen on the team as soon as possible and prove myself." I hand him the remote, unable to find anything worth putting on the TV.

"He's going to make us better this year." Keith's voice is full of excitement. "We are going to kick ass. I feel it in my bones."

I'm hopeful and optimistic about this upcoming season too. Last season, the team played harder than ever before, and we dominated. Sure, we no longer have some of our best players, but with the new talent, I'm hopeful we can make it to the Frozen Four college hockey championship again.

My focus will have to be split between myself and the team this year, while I try to impress scouts and secure a future with an NHL team. I won't admit it to anyone, but when I think about the pressure of playing, knowing scouts are watching, where every move I make could impact my future, I feel my stomach tighten, my hands grow clammy, and my throat starts to close.

The first thirty minutes of my "alone time" at the beach needs to be dedicated toward reviewing my notes. It'll help me recommend alternate captains. The other thirty minutes will be working through this new anxiety I have, which I'm still unsure how to really do.

"Want to watch Family Feud?" Keith asks, finally stopping on a channel. "It's my comfort show."

"Sure man," I chuckle, walking to the kitchen to get water.

I wish I had a comfort show. Or honestly, a comfort anything because nothing seems to help me unwind and deal with my stress lately. I need to put more effort into finding ways to handle it before the season starts and the real stress begins. I've done some research on meditation and think I need to give it more of a try. Some great players in the NHL seem to find it helps them. I really hope it helps me. Nothing has helped to ease my mind.

"Damn, I've already seen this episode," Keith complains before a loud laugh erupts from him. "Hurry up, Luc. The next round is about to get juicy!"

Chapter Four

Laur

My sore back didn't love the flight to the beach, but at least I wasn't five rows back where Blake, Tyler, and Keith were squished into one row. They looked like they could barely breathe. The flight felt so much longer than just two-and-a-half hours. My eyes kept threatening to close. I had to fight myself to stay awake on the plan to review all of Libby and Bren's top twenty candidates to join the marketing and PR team. Sadly, I didn't even get through them all.

When planning for this trip, I was giddy with excitement at the opportunity to have a relaxing, stress-free time. Bren and I easily convinced a group of guys from the hockey team to come. Once Lucas and Keith were onboard, Blake, Silas and Brooks were easily convinced. Tyler took no convincing. Brooks told Blaine about the trip, so we had to invite him too.

But now it seems like I'll have more work than I anticipated. At least I'll have multiple days of being out in the sun, tanning with the sparkling sand between my toes. Seeing Lucas without a shirt most of the trip doesn't sound too bad either.

The massive white trimmed front porch of Lucas' aunt's house comes into view as we turn into the excessively long driveway. There's even an overside porch swing. She graciously let us use her beach house in Gulf Shores free of charge. The elaborate structure more resembles a mansion rather than a simple beach house.

A grin spreads from ear to ear when my eyes fall to the glittering beach that is practically in the backyard. The beach reminds me of my childhood. My parents tried to take Nick and me every other year when we were kids. There's even a grill area, which is truthfully much more of a large outdoor kitchen and in-ground pool with lounge chairs and daybeds. Our own little slice of heaven.

My eyes widen as I walk through the garage and into the massive kitchen, complete with shiny high end appliances and a grand table that will definitely seat us all. The living room is decked out with tasteful upscale seaside decor complete with an oversized, white sectional sofa that I pray no one spills on.

"If anyone even thinks about trying to claim the master, you better think twice," Lucas yells as everyone scrambles into the house to claim a room. "And the room next to the master is off limits!"

"Why the room next to the master? Don't want anyone to hear me moaning your name every night?" I cheekily nudge him.

"It's for Ryder King, if he shows up," Lucas mumbles, running his hand through his hair. "But now that I think about it, maybe I shouldn't have picked the room right next to ours . . . It's one of the three with a king bed. Figured I would need to give him his own room."

"Wow, that's very kind of you, Captain," I tease. "Already saving the best for your new star player."

"Yeah, yeah," he breathes out. "We'll see."

He winks at me and grabs my hand, pulling me close. Inhaling his familiar scent of freshly laundered clothes mixed with sandalwood, citrus, and other woodsy scents, calms me—he smells and feels like home.

Delicately placing a kiss on my forehead, he leans in closer to whisper in my ear, "There's a very large, built-in bench in the master shower. Perfect for you to sit back with my head between your legs, tasting your pu—"

"Libby!" I shriek, cutting him off, not wanting anyone to hear his plans for me later and praying I can keep quiet enough. My face turns the color of a freshly ripe tomato.

"Why the long face, Lib?" I ask Libby, her lips turned down with a frown.

"I'm sharing a room with Mitchell," she complains, making a retching, gagging noise.

"I'm not that bad," Blaine protests as he comes down the stairs. "At least there's two queen size beds instead of one." He lowers his gaze, and his words barely reach my ears as he rubs at the back of his neck.

"Just don't bring anyone home," Libby mandates. Her pout turns into a demanding glare. "I refuse to deal with that."

"No promises, Lib," Blaine replies cooly. "I can't always plan for that."

Libby makes an exaggerated throwing up noise. Bren and Tyler come down the hallway.

"Tyler and I are sharing bunk beds. How fun!" Bren shrieks enthusiastically, coming into the living room. No hint of sarcasm detected. Unsurprisingly, Bren appears genuinely elated to be sharing bunk beds as a fresh college graduate. Her go-with-the-flow, bubbly attitude is the exact opposite of Libby's frustration.

"See Libby, at least we don't have bunk beds. Wouldn't want you to hear what I'm doing on the top bunk at night," Blaine remarks with a wink at Libby.

Libby winces in disgust.

My stomach rumbles, ready to finally eat something. "I'll start making the margs," I declare and clasp my hands together. "Lucas, can you start the grill while Bren and Libby unpack the food?"

Everyone starts moving, following my lead and moving outside. Maybe I need to give myself more credit for being a promising lead for the PR team.

"Laur," Lucas calls to me from outside, "is everyone here? Just trying to get a head count on burgers."

"Almost! Ryan just texted that he is thirty minutes out with Harlan and *the* Ryder King. I'm ready to fangirl," I joke playfully.

Lucas rolls his eyes at Libby and Sydney, who both squeal in excitement at the mention of Ryder's name. Sydney is one of Libby's best friends from her classes. We've recently recruited her to come to hockey games, but she cares much more about the players than the game.

Ryder King definitely merits some fangirling, but I'm already a fully dedicated fangirl to Lucas Donato.

"Don't worry," I assure Lucas. "It won't make me less of a dedicated Donato fangirl." Sauntering over to him, I kiss him passionately on the lips. His hands grip my hips, pinning my body against his.

"Focus on grilling our burgers and less on your girlfriend's mouth, Donato," Tyler bristles with impatience. "I'm fucking starving."

Out of nowhere, a lime flies out of Lucas' hand, hitting Tyler square in the nose.

"Your lucky margaritas aren't made with grapefruits, Barret," Lucas growls at Tyler.

A girlish giggle escapes me at Lucas' corny joke. Out of the corner of my eye, I spy another lime flying through the air again, this time from Tyler's hand. I catch it before it makes contact with Lucas.

"Stop wasting my limes, or you won't get any margaritas," I threaten, shaking my fist clenched around the lime.

Lucas lets out a low chuckle. "Barret can't have any until after a post-dinner workout anyways."

"Are you kidding me, bro?" Tyler complains with a drawn out grown.

"Your choice." Lucas tilts his head towards Tyler, raising both eyebrows. "But as your captain, I would recommend it. And as your friend, I would still recommend it." A stern look briefly crosses Lucas' face, before he turns back to ready the grill.

Waiting to make drinks didn't even cross my mind. Guilt warms my cheeks. I feel like such an idiot. I knew Lucas would take the vacation workout regime very seriously, but it never occurred to me that the rest of the team would be less dedicated or complain about it.

As soon as my pitcher of fresh margaritas is ready, Tyler greedily hands me glasses to fill. He snatches one for himself and downs half of it in one sip. Blaine and Keith lounge poolside. Neither of them fazed by the drinks, staying put in their seats.

Tyler's eyes find his willing victim in another senior, Blake. Tyler nods his head toward the drinks, encouraging Blake to go against the captain's recommendation with him. Blake takes a glass, toasting Tyler in solidarity.

Basking in the glorious warmth of the summer sun, the girls and I chat. Libby and Sydney haven't stopped spilling the newest tea.

About twenty minutes later, the delicious grill master calls out that the food is ready. Swaying sluggishly when I stand, I realize I've had two strong margaritas on an empty stomach. Talking with the girls distracted me, but at least I'm enjoying the vacation already.

"I bet he's really a playboy," Libby declares. Practically drooling at the thought of the new player. "You would think that, Libby," Syd rolls her eyes. "I doubt he is."

"With a face, name, and reputation for being the most sought after college hockey freshman, I have no doubt he is," Bren adds her take.

Tyler hands Blake another margarita, pouring one of himself too, while he chimes in to the Ryder King rumors. "I heard from a buddy of mine that he could have gone pro but wanted to play college for a year or two first."

Great. Now all the lushes are gossiping over our newest player. Too loudly to hear the creak of the front door. Too tipsy to notice the three new males arrive—one of which chuckles and saunters down the steps of the outdoor patio.

"You know, ladies—" a lilting voice calls "—and gentlemen too, you could just ask the *most sought after college hockey freshman of this season* whatever it is you want to know." Ryder drops his duffle back on the patio with a dramatic *thud*.

A gasp escapes Libby's lips as she takes in the dark eyed, black-haired newcomer. Despite his features, dark and mysterious doesn't describe him in the slightest. The air around him crackles with an energetic buzz.

His tousled, midnight hair swishes to one side, almost covering his eyes. Ryder is devilishly handsome mixed equally with boyish charm.

At eighteen, he is still a boy after all. But judging from the looks of thirst and lust on Libby and Sydney's faces, they don't seem to notice the same way I do. Even Bren looks him up and down, giving him much more than a once over.

The girls are not the only ones stuck in a daze. An eerie quiet surrounds us as the guys take in their new teammate. My mind drifts, starting to wonder if Tyler or Blaine could take Ryder in a fight. Ryder might be young, but his lean and agile muscles stretch over every inch of his body.

"Ryder, nice to see you again," Captain Smooth sails in trying to defuse the lust and tension in the air. "You're just in time for some food."

Libby's face tinges bright pink, and it's not from the sun. She shakes off the daze, whispering an embarrassed greeting as the guys all re-introduce themselves to Ryder. Most of them have met him before, but none of the girls have. Coach keeps it very hush-hush anytime a hot prospect visits, even from the PR and marketing team. Based on the single minute of interaction I just witnessed, I don't blame him one bit.

"Hi Ryder, nice to meet you I'm—"

Ryder interrupts me, "Lauren Bellinger. The captain's girlfriend, sister of the great Nick Bellinger and daughter of the legendary Nico Bellinger." He extends a hand out for me to shake. "Nice to meet you too."

My eyes go wide. He knows who I am. He must take it as a sign that I'm uncomfortable with him mentioning my deceased family.

"Sorry, I didn't mean to be insensitive." He scrambles for words. "They were both phenomenal players."

"No need to apologize," I mutter, understanding. "Thank you. You're right, they are."

"Word on the circuit is you aren't too bad yourself, King," Blaine cuts in. My eyes fly to him, gratitude softening their edges.

Blaine's eyes drift over Ryder with a hostile glare and a small snarl on his face, as if he's off-put by him. *Tread lightly, Blaine, you can't afford to fuck up this year if you want any chance of earning the respect of Lucas and Coach.*

Ryder smirks. "You've seen me play, Mitchell. Don't act like it's just a rumor."

Libby giggles like a schoolgirl at Ryder's reply. Finally Blaine found someone to give him a taste of his own medicine.

Chitchat breaks out as we sit down to eat our dinner. Lucas focuses his conversation solely on Ryder. Ever since we planned this beach trip, he's mentioned too many times to count that he needs to make a good impression on Ryder this weekend. He didn't like when I teased him earlier about it.

I argued that inviting a freshman to a small trip with the top upper-class hockey players on the team shows that enough. No sophomores were even invited. But what do I know about winning over men.

That remark earned me a few seductive whispers in my ear about how I was very talented at winning a certain male over.

"Thanks for dinner, Lucas!" Libby says as she helps to clear the dinner plates.

"What's on the agenda for tonight?" Bren asks, squirming in her seat with a frenetic excitement, "Please tell me it includes going to the beach bar I think I saw earlier while exploring the beach."

"Beach bar? I hope that means bikinis count as shirts," Tyler mutters.

A very audible "Ew" and "Gross" come from the girls at the table. I swear Tyler has become more and more of a fuckboy lately. I would expect a crass comment like that to come out of Blaine's mouth but not Tyler's.

"It was just a joke!" Tyler starts to defend himself.

"Well if you talk like that, none of the girls will be interested in you enough for it to matter anyways," I chirp, unable to hold my tongue.

"Damn. She's feisty, Donato," Ryder says with a laugh as he playfully shoves Lucas. "I'm down for a beach bar."

Part of me is very tempted to comment that he's not even of age. He wouldn't be able to come to the bar, but before I can say anything of the sort, Lucas starts to talk about a workout regime.

"I was planning to work out in about an hour. Some of you" —he scowls looking at Tyler and Blake— "don't seem to care enough and have started drinking already." A sigh escapes him, and he runs his hands through his hair. "But if anyone wants to join me, we can use the athletic club down the beach for weight training and run sprints in the sand for cardio."

"Perfect. I didn't get a full workout this morning before hitting the road," Ryder declares. He seems genuinely chipper about working out.

All the guys, except Tyler and Blake, agree to meet out back by the pool in an hour before heading over to the athletic club. Lucas hasn't said anything to Tyler but by the incredibly subtle hint of frustration in his gaze and the slight curl of his knuckles, I know he's pissed off. Tyler isn't setting a pristine example by getting tipsy and skipping workouts. Even if this is a vacation and the team technically doesn't have any mandatory scheduled workouts this week, it doesn't look good.

Finalizing the plan, we decide that the guys working out will meet us out at the bar after they've finished. I'm still curious how Ryder will get in, but that's a problem for later. Should Lucas even be allowing Ryder at bars when he can get in serious legal trouble? Before I can bring it up, he kisses me on the cheek and tells me he is going upstairs for a bit, hinting at him needing his alone time.

All the guys seem to be doing their own thing before their workout. Tyler and Blake crack beers by the pool. Ryder comes back from putting his stuff in his room shirtless with his abs on full display, all freaking eight of them. This kid must work out twenty times a day.

"Can we sit on the beach with some drinks and watch them do their sprints? Then head to the beach bar after?" Libby whispers in awe, drool practically spilling out of her mouth.

Her wide eyes are far from innocent as she takes in Ryder's body before he dives into the pool. A burst of laughter escapes me, quickly echoed by Bren's. Libby found a new obsession.

"How could we have missed it!" Libby groans as the girls get ready for the beach bar. Blake easily talked us into playing Kings Cup with him and Tyler. We were too engrossed in the drinking game; we didn't notice the rest of the guys working out on the beach.

"Don't worry, Lib." I smack my lips together putting a little bit of color on them. "I'm sure Lucas will have them working out every day we're here."

Libby's face lights up, a small squeal of enthusiasm slips through her lips. If Bren wasn't moving for her big girl job, Libby might give her a run for her money in the woo-girl department. My hands twist through my hair as I braid it to the side. I throw on a cover up over my bikini to pair with jean shorts.

Sand squishes between my toes walking down the beach to the bar. The warm air mixed with the sound of the waves crashing brings back memories of the beach with my family. Closing my eyes, images of Nick and me building sandcastles fill my head. Nick would instruct me on where the castle towers should go, always determined to build the biggest sandcastle on the beach. My eyes sting, tears threatening to come.

Shrieks from Libby break my trance as Tyler chases her along the beach like a pair of teenagers, both wobbly on their feet from alcohol. So much for the low-key night before getting back to reviewing applications tomorrow.

Tiki torches line the various vibrantly colored outdoor seating areas. A glass garage door opens into the bar and houses a small indoor area, decorated with the same tiki theme.

Tyler walks in with Libby thrown over his shoulder. Their laughter echoes throughout the massive open air venue, complete with multiple bars and even a DJ booth. He paints a coy smile on his face, turning on his charm before he apologizes to the mid-forties female bartender, who's furiously eyeing him and Libby. His allure works on her, and her annoyed glare melts away.

Sitting down at a bright blue table, I take in the beautiful sunset view. With the bar right up on the beachfront, I'm envious of having this immaculate view every night.

"Free shot from the bartender." Pride fills Tyler's voice from securing a few free drinks. He hands me one, but I shake my head. Everyone else but Bren gulps down the shots like water.

"Bar?" Bren asks, her tone noticeably melancholy—well at least noticeable to me. Realization washes over me that Bren's been unusually quiet. She flashes me a brittle smile. Something is off . . . she isn't her usual bubbly self. Grabbing her hand, we walk to the bar and look at the specialty drink menu.

"I'm feeling something fruity," Bren declares and lets out a long sigh. "I bet they have incredible Mai Tais at this place."

"What's wrong Brennie Bean?" A crease furrows between my brows.

"I just miss Liam. The distance is a bigger strain than I imagined. I knew it would be hard, but I didn't expect to feel so . . ." Bren pauses searching for the right word. "I'm not even sure how I feel. I just don't feel whole. It sounds silly . . ."

"It doesn't sound silly at all, Bren." I take her hand in mine, reassuring her. "You and Liam have been together a long time, it's understandable. I wish I could be more helpful."

"Two Mai Tais please," Bren orders, dropping my hand. "I'll be okay."

"As much as I hate that you're leaving, I'm sure that work will help a lot and be a great distraction. You are going to be so busy; the Red Wings are lucky to have you."

"Yeah, you're right." She takes a sharp inhale. "Work will help. I hope."

The bartender hands Bren two drinks in colorful glasses with tropical umbrellas.

"You know I hate coconut. I'll order something myself."

Bren lets out another big exhale before taking a long sip. "Guess I'm getting drunk today."

I order a strawberry daiquiri before we head back to the table, Bren carrying a drink in each hand.

"Damn, someone has the right idea," Tyler exclaims as Bren sits down next to him. They must have gone to another bar to get drinks while we were gone.

"Cheers," Bren grumbles, holding up a glass.

"To a great night," Libby exclaims. Everyone holds up their drinks to toast each other.

"What's the plan for this great night?" Blaine asks as the group of late arrivals strolls toward our table.

My eyes linger on Libby, and I swear I see a reflection of hunger in her eyes as she takes in Blaine with his button-down Hawaiian shirt fully open, showing off his well-defined abs and muscular torso. I've seen that look on her face many times since I've known her but never in regard to Blaine freaking Mitchell . . .

Chapter Five
Laur

My heart practically leaps out of my chest watching Lucas saunter over to our table in his black swim trunks and floral button-down shirt. His shirt flows open with several buttons left undone, showing off his delectable chest but not revealing his entire torso like Blaine.

"Oh, hello, Captain, didn't know I'd see this much of you at the bar," I tease, before kissing him softly.

"Too much?" Lucas cocks an eyebrow.

"The perfect amount for the public eye." My gaze runs the length of his enticing body again. "Anything more is for my eyes only," I whisper in his ear.

"Luc, you want anything?" Ryder calls, "Mitch and I are headed to the bar."

"I'll go with you," Lucas replies. Before he goes, he tries to kiss my disappointment away. I knew I'd have to share him a lot on this trip but I hate the time apart from him. It seems like he is getting on well with Ryder King at least. Surprisingly, Ryder seems to be keen on Mitchell, even after he was such an asshole when we arrived.

Bren pulls me into a conversation about application reviews, which admittedly I should be much more focused on, but my brain has been so overloaded, I needed this break. Tomorrow we'll multitask by tanning by the pool and selecting the final candidates to interview, then set up the video interviews for when we are back on campus.

I catch myself nibbling at my nails as nerves chew their way through me with each word from Bren. Hoping to ease my tension, I take the last sip of my drink. My responsibility when I get back to campus is going to dramatically increase.

Bren narrows her eyes at me, sensing my stress. "You're going to do an amazing job leading the PR and marketing crew, Laur." Bren places her hands on my shoulders, consoling me. "Just don't forget to have fun! Especially while we're at the beach."

Almost as if on cue, a drink decorated with a maraschino cherry and orange slice appears in front of me. Lucas takes his seat next to me, smiling broadly. My eyes grow wide with delight as the fruity drink hits my tastebuds.

"What is this deliciousness?" I demand, eagerly taking another drink.

He leans in close to my ear, placing a hand on my bare thigh below the table. With a raspy voice, he whispers, "Sex on the beach. I figured you might enjoy it. I know I certainly would."

Covering my mouth with my hand, I try to contain myself and keep from spitting out my drink at his unexpected answer. My cheeks heat desire mixed with embarrassment that our friends might overhear.

"Maybe if you're lucky, you'll get some of your own," I respond softly with a sheepish grin.

"I've never done that before." He runs his fingers along my thigh. The heat from my cheeks rushes to the space between my legs.

"Done what?" Libby interrupts from across the table. The color on my face deepens to scarlet.

"Skinny-dipped," Lucas replies smoothly while he still casually caresses my thigh. His ability to remain cool and calm never ceases to impress me. I would have tripped over my words in an attempt to come up with a reply.

Tyler snorts. "Seriously?"

"Yeah, seriously." Lucas gives a dismissive shrug.

"There are a million lakes in Michigan! How is that even possible?" Libby pries.

"I haven't either," I chime in.

"You both need to get out more," Bren mutters.

Have all our friends gone skinny-dipping? I never thought of Lucas and I as boring people but maybe in comparison to our friends apparently we aren't that adventurous.

"I've never done it," Ryder adds. "Didn't realize it was a requirement."

Unease lingers in the air around our now silent table from Ryder's confession. With his reputation, it takes everyone by surprise. He shrugs nonchalantly, taking another sip of his beer. "Anyways, what else do you guys do for fun besides skinny-dip in lakes?"

A fit of frantic laughter bursts from Libby. "You're so funny, Ryder," she croons, placing her head in her hand as she pines over him. "We like to dance. Do you dance?"

"Not really. But there isn't really dancing music at this bar anyways." Ryder glances around at the group, as if trying to will someone to change the topic.

"Well let's finish these drinks and dance in the sand!" Sydney shrieks, startling me. She's been so quiet I almost forgot she was there.

"One more round first!" Libby exclaims.

Tyler rises, joining Libby and Sydney to order one last drink. My pulse quickens as I catch his eye and raise an eyebrow at him as if asking him if he's sure he really needs another one.

Reluctantly, he sits back down at the table, telling Libby he's good on drinks.

A few of us leave the bar and meander down the beach back to the house. Blaine plays music off his tiny, but incredibly loud, portable speaker he brought in his pocket.

My heart beats rapidly again as Tyler makes his way to my side and signals for me to part from the group so we can talk. We veer off a little to talk in private.

"What was that look for back at the bar?" he snarls, his voice low and irritated.

A lump grows in my throat at the bite in his rude tone.

"Nothing," I answer quickly.

"Laur, that's a lie. I don't need you to mother me. I can hold my liquor, and we're on vacation—"

I cut him off. "You can do whatever you want, Ty, but, if you want to make alternate captain this year, maybe lay off a bit and don't miss any more workouts because you're too busy partying."

"Did Lucas—" He starts before I interrupt him again.

"Lucas didn't say anything. But as one of your closest friends, who knows how badly you want that 'A' on your jersey this year, it's just my personal opinion."

"Noted," Tyler mutters. My stomach twists with unease as an unfamiliar awkwardness falls between us as we drift back with the rest of the group. I'm used to being able to talk to Tyler about anything.

The discomfort doesn't last long. Sydney ambushes Tyler from behind, jumping on him, almost causing him to fall face first in the sand. Libby's hysterical laughter mixes with the music. She grabs Ryder's hand, trying to pull him to dance with her along the beach.

"I don't dance," he comments.

Libby pouts with zero subtly, kicking up sand like a child throwing a fit.

"C'mon, Ryder King," Blaine calls. "Live a little."

Blaine rushes forward, scooping up Libby and twirling her around as if the beach is a ballroom dance floor. Out of the corner of my eye, I spot movement from Lucas. He tries to be discreet, but I can tell he's ready to pounce. I take off running down the beach, with Lucas hot on my heels. Catching me easily, Lucas picks me up, spinning in circles. I squeal like a woo-girl. His speed could never be outmatched by mine.

"Is everyone on the team this cheesy?" Ryder grouses, making me giggle.

"What's cheesier than playing a game of truth or dare?" Sydney inquires, clearly hoping to keep the night going.

My stomach does a somersault at her suggestions. I absolutely despise the childish game. It brings back memories of my toxic ex and his friends. They got high off the game by daring each other to do the stupidest things while they were drinking, like running as hard as possible into the garage door with a hockey helmet on. Someone's mom was less thrilled than I was about that one—it cost her an entire new garage door.

"Aren't we a little old for that?" Blaine retorts. Bad boy Blaine Mitchell doesn't like truth or dare? Everyone seems to be full of surprises on this trip.

"Not even a little bit," Libby argues, crossing her arms. "It's a classic for any trip. What are you scared of Blaine?" She narrows her eyes at him, challenging him to back out.

"Whatever," Blaine grumbles as we approach the gate to the back patio.

Libby and Sydney bounce with giddiness, eager to play. They scurry into the house and return with a pack of hard seltzers. Bren says goodnight, mentioning she wants to take advantage of the empty room and call Liam before it gets too late.

"You first, Lib, since it was your idea," Tyler requests, earning him a groan from Libby.

"Technically it was Syd's idea, but whatever, Tyler. I'll be a good sport." Libby flashes a teasing grin, "I pick truth."

"Which guy on the team would you sleep with if you had to choose?" Silas Harlan, a junior defenseman, asks. Sydney bursts into a fit of giggles as she sips a seltzer she grabbed from the fridge.

"What a waste of a question, Harlan," Blaine grumbles. "We all know she's going to say Ryder. Next person."

Ryder shrugs unfazed by Blaine's comment. Harlan mutters "shit" under his breath, not realizing his obvious mistake. Before Libby gets a word out, Sydney starts with a new victim, locking her eyes on Blaine.

"Blaine, truth or dare?"

"Truth," he responds. Tyler huffs 'boring" under his breath. "Fine. Dare."

"I dare you to streak. One lap to the beach and back," Sydney challenges him.

"Easy." A cocky smirk forms across Blaine's face. "Just remember you asked for it."

Keeping his eyes focused on Libby, he takes off his Hawaiian shirt and works to untie his shorts.

"I'm going to get a drink," I stammer, not wanting to witness Blaine naked. I've already seen him in all his glory in the locker room last year. Before anyone can respond, my feet carry me quickly to the kitchen. I grab a cup of water, not wanting any more buzz than the slight one I currently have.

The sound of the sliding door opening alerts me that someone else has come inside. Turning, I expect to see Lucas but instead I'm greeted by Ryder King.

"Hey, Ryder." I take a long sip of my water.

"Hey. I'm headed to bed. Long travel day today," he offers. "And truth or dare isn't really my thing." He mumbles the last part so quietly I can barely make out the words. I wonder if it was more to himself than to me.

"I don't blame you," I laugh softly. "Just text Lucas if you need anything."

He acknowledges with a nod, then darts up the upstairs to his bedroom. Filling my water glass up again, a big sigh escapes me. Truth or dare is also not my thing. Nathan and his teammates at East used to force it on everyone at parties all the time his freshman year. It always became a pissing contest. But I continue to move on from the past, one day at a time.

"Laur, perfect timing," Libby calls to me as I close the door and make my way to Lucas on the patio. "It's your turn."

Great. Just what I was hoping to avoid.

"Since Blaine, everyone has picked truth. So please, provide us with more entertainment on our first night of vacation," Sydney pleads.

"Oh," My fingers nervously twirl a strand of hair. Despite the new knot in my stomach, I oblige, "Dare."

"I dare you to go skinny-dipping," Tyler proclaims loudly

"No way in hell is my girlfriend getting naked in front of my teammates," Lucas interrupts.

"Oh c'mon, it's just a game!" Libby squeals, "If it's that big of a deal she can go down to the beach and get naked there. Not like she needs to get buck-ass-naked right here like Blaine did."

"Blaine was right. We're too old for this shit," Lucas comments under his breath. A slight victory smile creeps along Blaine's lips.

"Why the hell not?" I state. Lucas' jaw tightens when I accept the stupid dare. "Like Libby said, I'll just go down by the beach and strip down there. Do we have any dry towels out here?"

Lucas clenches his fist as Blaine scrambles to find me a towel.

"Care to pop that skinny-dipping cherry with me, Captain?" My lip tingles as I not-so-subtly bite it. His fists unclench and a wicked grin replaces the tension that painted his face seconds ago.

"Well, this isn't fun anymore," Harlan groans, taking another hard seltzer from the open pack.

"Yep, I'm ready for bed. See you all tomorrow." Blaine leaves the patio.

A few guys linger behind with Sydney, chatting and drinking their seltzers. Clearly not taking anything I said to heart, Tyler is one of them.

"Let's cross skinny-dipping off the bucket list." Lucas grabs my hand, holding the towels in the other, as we run down the beach.

"Sorry to be possessive," Lucas starts as we get to the edge of the water.

"Don't be ridiculous. It's not like I want to be naked in front of our friends!" Pulling Lucas to me, I start to unbutton the rest of his shirt. "And I certainly don't want my friends or anyone for that matter drooling over you."

He flings his shirt into the sand. I pull my black swim cover up over my head, throwing it on the sand next to his shirt.

"I don't mind when you're possessive." I slide my shorts off. "If I'm being honest . . . it's kind of a turn on."

"Good."

"Good," I agree, untying my bikini top, letting it fall to the beach. Lucas eyes widen as he takes in my bare chest, my nipples hardening with the cool breeze.

"In that case," he growls against my lips before claiming them with his own as he takes off his boxers and swim trunks in one fell swoop. "You are mine."

Chapter Six

Lucas

The crash of the ocean waves creates a perfect song for our night—a soundtrack just for Laur and me. The idea of this moment has played on repeat in my head the last few hours ever since I mentioned never skinny dipping. Sure, it was a great way to throw off our friends from overhearing our intimate conversation, but it somehow worked in our favor much more than I expected.

My lips are still locked against hers as I pull her perfect body against mine, lightly dragging my fingers along her soft skin to the top of her red swimsuit bottoms that she still has on. Slowly, I trace the outline of them against her hips, toying with the little strings keeping it in place, causing Laur's body to shudder with anticipation.

"I'll take them off myself if you keep taking your sweet time," she threatens in my ear. A biting heat dances along my neck as her teeth meet the soft flesh, quickly soothed by the softness of her lips.

My knees hit the sand in front of her, slowly and sensually kissing along the fabric of her bikini bottoms. I slide my hand inside them. A quiet moan slips through Laur's lips when my fingers find her sweet bud. My thumb strokes her clit left to right, gradually increasing speed and pressure. More sounds of delight tumble from her mouth as friction builds between her legs. She squeezes her thighs together, squirming in pleasure. With my other hand, I untie one side of her bikini. My eyes trail the red fabric as it falls from her and onto the wet sand.

My desire is torn between wanting to continue to pleasure her and wanting to admire her standing fully naked on the beach. I effortlessly slide two fingers inside her tight slit. Her eagerness for me is evident in how slick and wet she is. My cock pulses in response. My tongue craves the musky, delicious taste of her desire. A low, quiet growl escapes me as I swipe my tongue across her center. It takes every single ounce of willpower not to devour her pussy right this second and send her into total bliss.

"I need to look at you," I tell her as I stand.

My cock twitches as my eyes fully take in every inch of her beauty. She's panting and out of breath. A wild longing clouds her blue eyes. I battle with my self-control, forcing myself not to automatically wrap my hand around my cock at the sight of her. I'm so in awe I can't help but lean in closer to her. The silver glow from the moon glistens against her perky bare breasts, while her dark hair delicately reflects the starlight, like a radiant goddess of the night sky.

"The moonlight suits you," I whisper against her lips before they lock with mine in a fervent, heated kiss.

"You suit me," she responds in a sultry and velvety voice.

"Yes, yes, you do."

"But . . ."

Pulling back, I raise an eyebrow at her. "But what?"

"As much as I want you to bend me over right here, right now," her tone is a low alluring whisper, each word laced with temptation. "We aren't completing our dare, and I am not someone who backs down from a challenge."

Before I can get a word out, Laur rushes into the water and starts to swim. A breathy exhale leaves me as I shake my head, baffled. My girl never ceases to surprise me. What a tease.

"You better swim fast. I'm coming for you!"

Laur's laughter and shrieks as I swim to catch her mix with the sound of the waves crashing against the beach, adding to the sound-track for the perfect summer night.

Once I catch up to Laur, she wraps her legs around me, our bodies intertwining in the water. Her nipples harden against my chest from the cool breeze, sending a pulse of desire through me.

Another squeal escapes Laur when I lift her legs higher around my waist so her tempting nipples are more easily accessible.

"Let me warm you up." My voice rumbles out as a low growl against her skin. A wanting sigh escapes her lips when I take her nipple into my warm mouth, flicking it with my tongue before softly sucking. She lets out a soft moan as I move to her other nipple.

My lips find the way to her neck, trailing kisses up to her ear before playfully nibbling on it. Letting out a deep exhale in her ear sends shivers down her spine.

"I want you." Each word out of Laur's mouth drips with longing as she tightens her legs around me.

Biting her neck playfully, I make my way to her alluring mouth.

"And I want you," I whisper against her soft lips. My kiss devours her, my lips eager and my mouth full of hunger.

"Not here," she pushes back. "I don't want to do it where all the sea creatures are."

Her face distorts into disgust and fear. I can't hold back my chuckle at her ridiculousness.

"Then let's go home, Laur."

Making my way out of the water with Laur still wrapped around me, I skim kisses along her neck and collarbone. My lips never leave her skin until we are on dry land.

I plant one more desperate kiss on her lips and set her down on the beach. The second my gaze falls to her wet naked body glistening in the moonlight, my cock starts to grow harder.

"Are you sure you want to wait until we get back to the house?" My voice is husky and frantic.

Her eyes drink me in, with a lingering stare. She roams every inch of my body, causing my cock to twitch. She notices, giving me a wicked smirk. *God.* I would do just about anything to give her a few inches right now.

"You don't want your cock to feel like it's being rubbed with sandpaper, do you?"

Instinctively, I place my hands on my cock imagining the discomfort.

"That's what I thought." Her soft giggle barely audible with the clamor of the ocean.

Wrapping a towel around herself, she tosses me the other but grabs my hand, pulling me to follow her before I can wrap it around myself.

"Hurry!" she commands, dropping my hand and dashing towards the house. "Don't make me wait!"

Scrambling in the sand, I wrap my towel around myself and find our clothes before running to the house as quickly as my feet will take me after her. My gaze instantly falls to the luscious daybed on the very deserted back patio. Tilting my head in the direction of the daybed, I raise my eyebrows at Laur.

"Out here?" Laur asks, her voice quiet, shy. "What if someone sees us?"

"Everyone is asleep," I reassure her, sitting down on the daybed. "We already crossed public indecency off the list tonight."

Without another word, Laur drops her towel by the pool and struts over to me.

"Have it your way, Captain," she purrs as yanks off my towel and straddles my lap.

"Oh, I will." Lifting her up, I flip her over so she's on her back, looking up at me. My head finds its favorite spot between her thighs. "I didn't get to finish having this my way."

My tongue swipes her center, my cock hardening at the taste of her pussy on my tongue. Gently pulling her clit into my mouth, I suck and flick my tongue against her bud, while two fingers find her entrance. I feel her slicken further for me with each lick and suck while my fingers pump in and out of her. Her hand flies to her mouth to muffle her cries of pleasure.

"You're going to get us caught," she pants.

"*I'm* being quiet," I tease as I find her familiar, glorious, sweet spot with my fingers causing a loud, raspy moan to break free from her lips.

"We." She places both hands over her mouth, attempting to stifle her sounds.

"Need to." She can't get the words out.

"Go inside." Her walls tighten, gripping my hand as she comes close to her release.

"Not yet." My gaze falls to her body, want dancing in my eyes.

Taking her clit to my mouth again, I run my tongue back and forth in a fast flicking motion. My fingers hitting her g-spot over and over and over. She pulses against them letting out a loud cry of ecstasy as she finds her release.

She releases a whimper when I pull my fingers from her pussy. I drink in the sight of her cum gleaming in the moonlight on my hand. With a devilish smirk, I suck her arousal off my dripping fingers. "Now we can go inside." I grab one of the towels, wrapping it tightly around my waist but it does little to mask my bulge.

"Good," she pants, wrapping herself up in the other towel, "because I need you inside me. Now."

In a blink of an eye, Laur darts into the house and sprints up the stairs to our bedroom. I'm hot on her heels. The second the bedroom door closes, she dramatically lets her towel fall to the floor before strutting over to me and pulling mine off.

"You are very ready for me," she purrs. Hunger grows in her eyes as they linger on my rock hard cock.

With a devilish grin, I take my cock in my hand, gently stroking myself but never letting my eyes leave hers. Her tongue traces her bottom lip, causing my dick to twitch. Desire fills the air around us, coyness gleaming in her baby blues as she lays down on the bed and spreads her legs, eagerly waiting for me.

Prowling onto the bed, I close the space between us and slide myself between her thighs. A grunt of ecstasy escapes me as I push into her dripping wet heat in one swift, hard thrust. *Mmm*. She is very ready for me too. Laur's hand flies to her mouth to suppress the moan that instantly spills from her mouth.

"Shhhh," I whisper. My hips shoot forward, plunging my cock deeper in her pussy, the devilish smile still etched on my face. "We have to be quiet."

I begin pumping in and out of her, the headboard loudly thudding against the wall with each thrust of my hips. Between the headboard and Laur's terrible attempts at staying silent, someone is going to hear us. Trying to muffle the sound, I place one hand on the headboard and one hand on her hips, but the noisy headboard thunders louder.

"Get on your knees," I demand in a husky voice. "Put your hands on the headboard."

"Kinky," Laur whispers breathlessly.

In truth, it's more so we can force the headboard against the wall instead of me trying to be sexy, but she doesn't have to know that.

Kneeling behind her, I line the head of my cock with her opening, entering her from behind. My head finds the crease in her neck, biting her neck as I bury myself deep inside her.

My fingers intertwine with hers, pushing the headboard back. Her hand no longer covering her mouth, Laur's cries of pleasure fill the room.

"You're so tight," I growl against her ear.

She rocks her hips back to meet mine, and I groan in response. Her soft skin presses against my chest as she arches her back, causing me to plunge deeper inside her, so close to filling her.

Taking one hand from the headboard, my hand finds her clit. She moans my name, biting her lip hard to keep quiet. With two fingers, I move quickly back and forth as I drive into her again and again until she's quivering. The instant her walls spasm around my cock, I find my release, filling her. I watch in pure satisfaction as my cum slowly trickles down the inside of her thigh as I slip my cock free.

"Holy shit," I pant, laying down on the bed.

"Yeah." Laur giggles breathlessly, laying her head on my chest. "Holy shit is right."

When I wake up, Laur's naked body is entangled with mine and the sheets of our bed.

"Good morning, pretty girl." I kiss her cheek before getting out of bed to brush my teeth and shower after last night's post skinny-dipping escapades.

"I'm glad we avoided sex on the beach. I don't want sand in all my crevices. No, thank you!" Laur yawns widely. "Anyways, I'm headed downstairs to start some coffee."

My chuckle echo against the shower walls at her random remark. She always keeps me on my toes. The warm water washes away the sinful night.

After my shower, I quickly tiptoe to lock the bedroom door. I don't want Laur to walk in on me. But any of the others walking in on me would be much worse . . .I don't know if I could face them confidently after.

I wrap my towel tightly around my waist, take a seat on the floor, and open my meditation app. I need to start with a clear, stress-free mind today. If meditation works for Alex Killorn to better his NHL—then I'll give it a try. I'm giving meditation a try. I need to find something to help manage my higher stress levels.

The scent of freshly brewed coffee fills the air. It's barely 8:00 a.m., and I find Laur and Bren alone in the kitchen. Laur sips her coffee as she scribbles frantically on what I assume are applications for their PR and marketing team. Being a leader on different hockey teams has been a constant throughout my life, but running a program and making that team look good is a very different kind of pressure I don't think I could handle. Laur will be phenomenal at it; she already is.

"Morning, Lucas!" Bren greets, sitting next to Laur with her own stack of potential candidate resumes.

"Good morning," I reply while grabbing a coffee mug off the counter. "Been up long?"

"You know I'm a morning person just like you," Bren says, taking a big sip of her coffee. "I'm surprised you slept in."

"Blame Laur," I tease, which earns me an eyeroll from Laur before she turns back to her notes again. "I'm headed back upstairs to review some player notes, just needed to grab coffee."

Sitting at the desk in my room, I thumb through some NHL news before I review some of my team notes. Inspired by Nick Bellinger's notebook on rival teams and players, I created my own.

It seemed rude at first, writing about my teammates, their strong skills and where they could make improvements, especially because some of them are my closest friends. I don't have much written down yet, but I'm hoping to spend some time each week jotting things down to strengthen our team.

Playing for the NHL after college has been my lifelong team, which means being captain and pushing myself and the Wyverns to go above and beyond this year is crucial.

The journal on the team is strictly for my eyes, and only about hockey. I read online it could be helpful to write down other things—conflicts, irritations, observations—to help with my stress but that feels too dramatic and too close to the journaling for therapy.

Aside from Blaine Mitchell and his goonies' delinquent behavior, there isn't much conflict surprisingly, and he has toned it down significantly since the end of last season, so much that I don't want to knock his teeth in every time he talks.

I'm the "levelheaded, has his shit together" captain. I'm not about to write down my feelings for anyone to find. Regardless, the notes on players' strengths and weak spots will be helpful down the road.

If I was writing about my irritations . . . I would furiously write how ridiculous it is Tyler got shit-faced yesterday instead of working out when Ryder King got here. Tyler played it coy, but I saw him constantly taking shots with Libby. He was drunk the entire day.

Yeah, I know I'm not great at relaxing and that this is a vacation, but we still need to make a good impression on King to show the team is a damn good time. If he wants my recommendation as alternate captain to Coach, he's going to have to prove he can be a great leader and get really good at sweating out his hangover. Starting today.

Mitchell has surprised me though. He seems to keep surprising everyone. At first, I thought he would punch King in the face—in typical Mitchell fashion—but after the initial introduction, they seemed to be getting along fine. Hell, they were even chatting at the bar.

One of my old hockey nets is in the garage and the guys that drove down brought some sticks and pucks along. I'm eager to get back to campus to see Ryder on the ice, but shooting in the driveway will have to do for now.

King's fierce. I've watched and re-watched videos of him playing. Working out yesterday, King's drive and energy seemed to be contagious. Mitchell hit a personal record with pull-ups yesterday when Ryder kept telling him to push through the pain. It might have been more Mitchell wanting to get more reps than King, but whatever the motivation was, it still got Mitchell working harder. And that was just one day in the gym. I'm already imagining them feeding off each other on the ice.

"Lucas, breakfast is almost ready!" Laur calls from downstairs.

Glancing at the clock, I see it's already nine. Everyone's probably awake by now.

"Scrambled okay, Lucas?" Bren calls from the stove as I walk into the kitchen. She's a phenomenal cook, and I worry for our friend group after she leaves for her new marketing job. I don't think any of us have ever cooked for more than two people besides Bren.

"Yeah, that's great. Thanks, Bren!"

Laur's chatting with Tyler and King. She smiles at me and sips a piping hot cup of coffee, steam still rising from the cup. I'd bet money that's at least her third now—she is a terrible morning person.

"The room and everything okay, Ryder," I ask, taking the seat next to him at the kitchen table. Everyone is spread out between the kitchen and living room for breakfast.

"Yeah, I slept great but not as good as you did," he retorts with a sly grin.

My eyes widen and Laur's face instantly turns scarlet red in the seat across from me. Shit. Maybe the beach would have been a better idea.

"Oh my gosh . . . We are so sorry," Laur starts before King cuts her off with a laugh.

"It's no big deal." He chuckles. "I'm just giving you shit."

"Did you seriously hear them going at it last night?" Libby giggles from the couch next to Sydney.

"What are you laughing about? I heard you too." Ryder calls Libby out. Her face pales to a ghostly white and a stunned gaze fills her eyes.

"What?" a shriek of excitement or confusion—truthfully, I'm not sure which—erupts from Sydney. "LIBBY! I've been sitting next to you for at least twenty minutes, and you haven't said a word? What kind of best friend are you!"

"It's not a big deal . . ." Libby looks away, avoiding making eye contact with every single person here.

"Wait, but Mitchell was sleeping on the daybed by the pool this morning," Conner pipes in. "So who was it?"

Libby's face turns almost translucent as she exchanges a glance with Mitchell.

"It was me," Mitchell stutters with embarrassment. "But I woke up at 5:00 a.m., unable to fall back asleep." He casually shrugs as if this conversation is no big deal. "Didn't want to keep her awake."

"I can confirm when Lucas and I came in last night, he wasn't out there," Laur interjects.

Thank fucking God. If Blaine was out there while we were on the beach, I would have lost my shit.

"Okay," Bren says slowly. "Before this gets any weirder . . . who wants breakfast?"

Chapter Seven
Blaine Mitchell

Why did I just lie and cover for Libby that I was the one she hooked up with last night? It makes absolutely no sense. But the second her Bambi eyes and panic-stricken face met mine, the fib easily rolled off my tongue. She was signaling she needed me. But I have no idea why.

My mind races as I scarf down my delicious breakfast of eggs, bacon, and toast in silence. At breakfast, Sydney kept attempting to subtly get details out of Libby about last night, but she stormed out of the room without even touching her breakfast. Excusing myself from the table, I put my dishes in the sink to go check on her.

Knock. Knock.

"Lib, it's me. Can I come in?" I'm not sure why I knocked on the door. We're sharing a room and it's not locked, but I have no idea what in the world is happening right now. My stomach turns, waiting for her to respond.

Libby swiftly opens the door and yanks me inside, closing it quickly but quietly.

"Did you tell them?" she asks, her eyes wide as she nervously bites her fingernail.

"Tell them what?"

"Did you tell them that you lied? That we didn't hook up? That it wasn't you?"

"No." My hands are clammy. Why am I so nervous? I'm not lying to Libby. I'm lying to every single person on this trip but her.

"Why not?" Libby questions in a hushed tone.

"Libby, c'mon. What the fuck is going on?" I demand.

"Nothing!"

"Who was it?" I question. It has to be someone she's embarrassed about, but they would know she lied. It doesn't make any sense.

"No one here, I swear," she sheepishly whispers.

"Then why did you telepathically tell me to say it was me? That makes no fucking sense."

"I know, I know. It's complicated. Blaine, please. Just keep the secret. I promise I'll owe you. Everyone thinks it's you anyways, it's not a big deal. Right?"

"Libby, I- don't know."

Everyone thinking I hooked up with Libby isn't going to do me any favors. I need to rebuild my reputation. I can't be seen as the bad boy if I want any chance of making alternate captain before I graduate in two years. I just started becoming part of the inner circle. Lucas doesn't seem to hate me anymore. Ryder King and I surprisingly get along. Libby's distressing pleas derail my thoughts.

"Blaine, I'm begging you to keep the truth between us. I know it's a lot to ask." Her eyes are as big as saucers, with tears threatening to fall any second. She's shaking slightly like she might break into pieces.

"Okay." I stumble over my words. My heart can't take seeing her, or any woman for that matter, about to fall apart. "Sure, Lib. Just tell me everything is okay. No one hurt you, did they?"

"No, NO! I promise it is nothing like that. Thank you. I owe you." She throws herself into my arms, squeezing me tightly. I wrap my arms around her, still not understanding the situation but understanding she needs me for some reason.

"Thank you," she whispers again. "You're a good friend."

Tears stream down her face. She pulls away from me and rushes out the door without another word and into the bathroom down the hall.

What the hell am I about to get myself into?

Chapter Eight

Laur

Coffee stains my sweatshirt from breakfast when Blaine and Libby confessed to being together last night. Luckily, I had just taken a sip and my coffee cup was still pressed to my mouth, so no one, aside from my brand new sweatshirt, noticed my subtle spit take.

Shocking doesn't even begin to describe the news. Truthfully, it always seemed like Libby was interested in Tyler. Just because I'm starting to warm up to Blaine doesn't mean I want to see the trouble-maker of the hockey team sleeping with one of my best friends. But maybe she could keep him in line, and he could keep her from her habit of one night stands too.

One thing is for sure: I might have to tape my mouth shut to keep myself from grilling Libby while we finalize our first round of inter-views. Millions of questions swirl in my head: when did it start? How? Was this the first time? Is it just sex? How good was it? It had to have been good . . . Sure I've seen glimpses of him naked, but anyone who has ever been within a foot of Mitchell when a girl is around knows how smooth he is. The words will never come out of my mouth around Tyler, but girls flock to him more than they flock to Tyler and that's saying something. Girls are drawn to him. I guess everyone loves a bad boy.

Stacks of paper, notepads and laptops cover the kitchen table just minutes after we finish eating. The guys already headed off to workout before messing around with Lucas' old hockey equipment. I'm not sure if Blaine went with them. I haven't seen him or Libby after they abruptly left breakfast.

I'm sure Tyler is in for a great time with his pale face and bloodshot eyes. He'd clearly shown all the signs of his hangover at breakfast, slumped over with exhaustion.

Not wanting to interrupt Libby and Blaine, I shoot her a text that we need to get moving on solidifying the first-round interviewees or we won't get any more free time on this trip.

A few minutes later, Libby comes into the living room where Bren and I are sitting. Her eyes have a slight puffiness to them, like she'd been crying. My heart throbs with sorrow not knowing what is going on with her.

"You okay, Lib?" I ask, risking sounding like the mom figure, which is typically Bren's role to play.

"Yeah, I'm fine." Libby retorts quietly.

"Are you sure? You know you can talk—" I start, but she cuts me off.

"I know, I know. I really am fine." She sounds more like her chipper self. "I just don't want to talk about it. If I do, I promise I will come to you or Syd."

"Can I just ask one thing?" Sydney inquires from the opposite couch where she's been quietly lurking, earning her a stern look of frustration from Libby.

"Fine," Libby snaps back.

Looking from left to right to ensure all the boys are truly out of the house, a mischievous grin forms on Syd's face. "Are the rumors true?"

"What are you talking about?" Libby questions, her voice rising at the end.

"You know . . ." Syd suggestively raises her eyebrows a few times. "Is he really thicker than a fist?"

Thank goodness I'm not drinking coffee right now, I would have spewed it everywhere.

"People really say that?" Bren asks.

Syd nods profusely. "Oh girls say many, many things about many, many parts of Blaine Mitchell."

Glad I'm not part of that rumor mill. I don't need to know details about any of the hockey team's sexual escapades or body parts—only Lucas.'

"Well . . ." Sydney taps her fingers on her coffee mug impatiently waiting for Libby to respond. She clearly is not going to let up. She practically bounces on the couch with anticipation.

A big sigh escapes Libby before she replies, "Biggest I've ever seen." A shy smile paints her face. "Now, no more questions. From any of you."

Bren's wide eyes and shocked expression mirrors mine.

"Uhm . . . okay." My cheeks heat at the conversation. "Let's get to work then."

"Yeah, enough about Blaine Mitchell's dick," Bren giggles, "and more about the best new girls to help promote it."

"BRENNA!" My yell gets lost in the laughter that fills the kitchen from Bren and Syd. Even Libby lets out a chuckle at Bren's ridiculous remark.

"I've got some good contenders," Libby mutters.

"Me too!" Syd snorts, still in a giggle fit on the couch.

"Enough from you, Sydney!" I pipe up "Let us work! I'm going first. I will back this girl one hundred and ten percent. Her name is Lena."

"She looks familiar," Bren says, squinting at the photo attached to the application.

"Bren, I've known you for over twenty-one years. You've said that about stock photos in picture frames before," I reply.

"True." She sighs into her coffee. "Carry on."

I start to run through the details. "Lena ran the social media account for her high school's hockey and soccer teams."

"I love the sample content she provided," Bren interjects. "It's witty and really engaging. She'd be the content queen for the team."

"Right? That's what I was thinking!" I beam. "She even has experience coordinating the soccer team's charity gala every year. Major points for that. We need some new fundraising ideas."

Truthfully, I'm hoping for something unique and original since the Bellinger special edition jerseys were such a success this year. Lena is an incoming freshman, which is great since she would stay longer term. She's the perfect candidate.

Within a few hours, we have three more applications to review and a handful more spots to fill for interviews. The "maybe" pile is rather massive, so we broke it into a "maybe yes" and a "maybe-probably not" pile. A better system would be ideal, but for now we are just rolling with the punches.

"I'm on the fence about the next girl," Libby begins to explain as a few guys walk into the kitchen, interrupting her train of thought.

"On the fence about who?" Blaine asks.

"We can't disclose information until the interviews are done. Blaine, get out of here." Libby huffs at him with irritation.

"You've been gone a long time. We got a lot done!" I tell Lucas as he comes to greet me.

Lucas kisses me on the cheek, sweat dripping from his forehead and almost landing on my face. "We played some basketball after the gym."

"Which Donato sucks at, by the way." Ryder chuckles, dropping his bag in the living room.

"He's much better on skates." Tyler raids the fridge, looking for something to snack on and settling on some string cheese.

"Fuck off," Lucas jokes, snagging Tyler's unopened string cheese. "We're going to chill in the pool for a little bit before we mess around with my old hockey equipment. Any ideas on dinner?"

"What about a friendly competition for dinner? Then shooting drills after?" Ryder smirks.

"What did you have in mind?" Lucas raises an eyebrow.

"Have you heard of the show *Chopped?*" Ryder asks.

An uncharacteristic squeal slips past my lips. "My mom and I love that show!!"

Ryder explains in depth how his mom is obsessed with the cooking TV show that I have seen probably every episode of. There is a secret ingredient that all teams need to add somewhere into their meals, which includes a main dish and at least one side, but they don't know until after they get all of their other ingredients. He suggests we set a budget and have teams shop for ingredients for dinner not knowing what the mystery ingredient will be.

"The girls would be the judges then?" Blaine questions. "We would need to make sure they don't know who made what, so it's not biased."

"No offense, Laur, but we know you'd vote for Lucas," Tyler jests. "Some of the guys could be judges too. What if we just do three teams of two."

"I do love a man who can cook . . ." I remark, batting my baby blues in Lucas' direction.

Lucas eyes narrow, putting his steely game face on, so serious about this little competition now. "What if we go to the store in about an hour?" he asks, and I nod my head in response.

"That should give us enough time to wrap up what we need to for the PR and marketing team," I confirm.

"Great." Lucas smiles. "I promise you we don't want Keith cooking. He can get the secret ingredient with whoever else isn't cooking."

Eagerly, they rush into the backyard. They shout and divulge the details to the rest of our friends. Ryder bounces with a gleeful grin, his arms flailing with enthusiasm as he explains the rules. It reminds me of a little kid sharing a story. Who knew they would get this ecstatic about a cooking competition.

"This is going to be entertaining," Bren says. "I can't wait to tell Liam about who the worst cooks are. He would definitely be with Keith on special ingredient duty. I miss him . . ."

"I know you do." I grab Bren's hand and squeeze it firmly. "What if we FaceTime him later while the guys are cooking?"

She gives a weary sigh. "I'm sure he's busy, but we can try. Let's get back to the applications."

"Right," Libby picks up where she left off. "So this girl I am on the fence about." She hands me the application.

"Hold on, isn't this the girl you were all about before we left? We talked about her. No hockey ties but amazing charity event experience?"

"Yeah, Raven," Libby attests. "I'm not sure though. Something just seems off about her."

"She looks familiar . . ." Bren tilts her head slightly.

I roll my eyes in response. "We already established that someone looking familiar to you means nothing! What are you on the fence about?"

"Something just feels weird, I'm not sure," Libby tries to clarify.

"But her experience?" I flip through her application again.

"Is what we need," Bren declares, "or what *you* will need. This year is going to be really important to try to do some type of new charity fundraiser."

"Exactly. She has that expertise."

"If you're sure . . ." Libby's eyes dart back and forth between Bren and me.

My stomach knots at her apprehensiveness over selecting this girl to interview.

"If something is off with her, we'll find out when she interviews," I justify, trying to calm my new nerves. "But we need this type of skill on our team, so fingers crossed she interviews well."

"I think she will be an asset," Bren affirms.

There is one last spot for our first-round interviews to fill. Delight replaces the worry in my gut knowing we are in the home stretch and one step closer to finalizing the group of newbies that will support the hockey team this year.

"Hey, can we interrupt?" Ryder interjects from the patio. "We need help with figuring out what the teams are."

Bren rolls her eyes. "These boys, they can't do anything without us."

"We can play hockey!" Blaine retorts, while a few others mutter disapproval at Bren's comment.

"But you won't look as good to the outside world without us," Libby scoffs.

"Touché! Now help us!" Blaine jokingly brings his hands together, pleading for help.

As I jot down the names of the eight guys that are going to participate, Libby instructs Blaine to give her his hat.

"Ew," she scoffs. "It's sweaty." Blaine tuts his tongue at her as she puts the eight folded up pieces of paper in the hat. "Ryder, as the newest member of the hockey team you pick first."

"Tyler," Ryder reads off the name on the paper. "Wait, what if someone pulls my name? How does that work?" He furrows his brow in confusion.

"Easy," Bren takes the hat from Ryder and goes through the names, removing one slip.

"See this is why you would be lost without us," Libby giggles.

Blaine ends up picking Lucas' name, which leaves Blake Hursh and Silas Harlan as the last team.

"Don't forget to text Keith the secret ingredient!" Ryder calls to us as the boys scramble off to the store.

"I know we need to choose one last interviewee, but what should the ingredient be?" Libby whispers as if they are still in the house.

"I have an idea!" Syd jumps off the couch and rushes over to the kitchen table.

Chapter Nine

Lucas

Alittle friendly competition between teammates is healthy. Did I expect it to be cooking related? Absolutely not. I expected it to be around shooting in the driveway, but at least there's creativity and excitement from the guys. Ryder seems to have that quality; he's a catalyst for raring up the team with energy and enthusiasm. If it translates to the ice, he is going to be the biggest asset for the Wyverns this year.

Blaine and I dart around the grocery store, snagging our ingredients. I regret not having one of the girls come along to film how ridiculous we are all being—dashing in and out of aisles, tossing things into our carts like we set some sort of time limit, which I guess we probably should have. After fifteen minutes, I text Keith to give us a time warning or we will never leave this store.

"Five minutes!" Keith's voice bellows from the aisle over. A small elderly woman shopping next to us jumps at the sound of his voice booming through the store.

"Donato, I don't know if all these things go together," Blaine admits to me as he rifles through the items I've thrown into our cart. "Can I swap a few things out?"

My eyebrows raise at Blaine asking for my permission and his potential expertise with ingredients. "Yeah, man, go for it."

Back at the house, it's game on. The chef teams are scrambling to unpack their groceries and claim space in the kitchen before the girls divulge the secret ingredient.

"What if we all need to use the stove at the same time?" Tyler complains. "Who gets priority?"

"There's one outside too. There's enough space," I reply sharply, slightly annoyed with his lack of comradery.

"What about the oven?" Harlan interjects.

"We'll share the space. We share the ice almost every damn day," Blaine chimes in nonchalantly. "It's not going to be a big deal."

Pride swells in my chest at Blaine's team mentality, especially knowing how competitive and hotheaded he can get. Of course I want to win to show off for Laur, especially since she shared she loves to watch the show Ryder based this fiasco off of with her mom, but I wasn't keen to be partnered with him at first.

"It's just for fun," Ryder pipes up with the same vibrant energy he seems to always have.

"And to feed us," Libby retorts, her lip curled with slight disdain. "Please make something edible."

"That's not very likely, and I'm already starving," Bren mutters under her breath.

Blaine clears his throat in response. "You'll be delighted to know that Lucas and I took the liberty of preparing some appetizers for you all, since it's going to take us probably two hours to cook."

"We did?" I ask at the same time Libby whines, "Two hours?!"

Blaine proudly presents a tray with tortilla chips, various salsas, a chunky guacamole, and even a white queso dip as the appetizer we supposedly prepared.

"Swift thinking," I mutter to Blaine, patting him on the back. I wonder if his kind gesture has anything to do with his new situation with Libby.

A pleased grin appears on Blaine's face, which grows to a full ear to ear smile when Bren declares, "Five points for Lucas and Blaine. Not all heroes wear capes, but they understand a girl's love for queso."

"That's fucking ridiculous!" Tyler throws his hands up in frustration. "You can't give them points!"

"How do the points even work?" Blaine mumbles.

"Tyler, relax," Lauren speaks up, trying to save the day. "Bren was just joking around. We will judge fair and square. We'll even come up with our own point system while you all are cooking."

"Will Keith and Brooks bring out the food, so you don't know who it's from?" Tyler brows are drawn together as if he's a kid waiting for his parents to give him a serious answer whether his buddy can sleep over tonight.

"For fuck's sake, Tyler," Libby takes over. "Yes. Keith and Brooks will bring out the food. We will be drafting emails and eating the delicious snacks that Blaine and Lucas so thoughtfully brought. We can go somewhere else in the house if it's really that big of a deal." Hands on her hips, lips pressed together, Libby just scolded Tyler exactly like he was that little kid.

Tyler just nods in response, eyes filled with shock at Libby's response. He knows he is pushing his limits.

"Great, so now that we have that settled," Laur pipes up. "You will all have two hours to cook and plate your foods. You must ensure that the meal consists of a main course and at least one side dish, as previously agreed upon. Are you ready to know the mystery ingredient?"

"YES!" Blaine and Ryder shout in perfect unison. They are both hyped up for this game. Maybe we should integrate more little competitions off the ice throughout the season. Well . . . if this one goes well and Tyler can keep his shit together.

"The mystery ingredient is . . ." Libby drums on the counter for her big reveal. "Dried apricots! Keith, please disperse the ingredients to each team. Each team must use at least half of the quantity they are given!"

"Since when?" Blake asks as Tyler mutters, "Dried apricots? I thought it would be something like garlic or lemon."

"Since now, we said we would make up the rules while you cooked, didn't we?" Bren retorts, pulling her camera out to take video footage. "Tyler, are you aware that garlic and lemon are frequently used in standard recipes. This is supposed to be creative!"

"Hey, paparazzi, since when do I have time to learn whatever you consider to be a standard recipe?" Tyler swats at the camera jokingly.

"Well, boys, get cooking. Your two hours starts—NOW!" Bren declares.

Frantically, we all scramble to our claimed spots around the kitchen. Hushed voices fill the room as everyone discusses what they need to get started with their counterpart.

"Good luck!" Laur calls from the stairs as the girls go upstairs to finish working on . . . well whatever they are working on. Truthfully, I can't even remember, my blood is rushing and I'm getting caught up in excitement.

"Luc, do you trust me?" Blaine asks.

Scratching the back of my neck, I tilt my head in confusion. This conversation could go a lot of different ways. "In general?" I question.

"In general, would be great, but for now, I mean with cooking."

"Oh yeah, dude, sure," I confirm.

"Then let me take the lead on this. I have the perfect idea."

"You're the captain in the kitchen today." I nod in agreement. "I can cook about five things, and I don't think I have ever eaten an apricot in my life."

"It's called head chef, not captain," Blaine chortles, "but I'll take it. We got this in the bag."

I'm really hoping he's right. Winning this little competition would win me big points with Laur.

Chapter Ten

Laur

Rambunctious shouts and profanities drift upstairs from the kitchen while the girls and I finalize our interview schedule. Hilarious is an understatement hearing these hockey players in their twenties threatening to throw elbows over counter space and cooking utensils. I expected Lucas, being the wholesome captain that he is, to attempt to keep the peace for as long as possible. But the moment I hear "Blake, fucking move now" louder than any remark the guys have made so far, I know he's playing to win.

Bren sneaks downstairs a few times to spy on the boys and capture more videos to send to Liam, which we'll also secretly use for content on the hockey team's social media pages later. Each time, she's met with loud frustrated shouts reprimanding her to go back upstairs.

Keith is equally invested in his job as timekeeper, giving the teams updates that are so loud they drift up stairs so we can hear when one hour, thirty minutes, and ten minutes are left. I picture him pacing around the kitchen like a drill sergeant but with a spoon in hand.

"FIVE MINUTES LEFT, GENTLEMAN!" Keith's voice carries up the staircase along with the sound of Blake cussing up a storm. That doesn't sound promising.

"Done!" Libby exclaims as she hits send on the last email to our interview candidates. Nerves knot my stomach knowing that Bren moves on to her "big girl job" next week and I will be left to lead first round interviews in a very tight timespan. Interviewing any player from the hockey team live sounds less nerve racking.

"ONE MINUTE LEFT!" Keith bellows before he trudges loudly up the stairs, knocking politely on the door.

"Come in," Libby responds.

"Hi, ladies," Keith starts, a slight blush on his face. "Want to come down to the patio in fifteen minutes or so?"

"I thought they only had one minute left—" Bren raises her eyebrows, giggles erupting from her "—which is probably already up."

"Trust me, some of them need the extra time." Keith laughs. "Make sure you check that any chicken is cooked all the way before you take a bite . . ." Keith turns to leave, muttering. "The last thing we need is anyone getting food poisoning at the end of the trip."

Wonderful. Who doesn't love salmonella?

The house is eerily quiet as we walk down the stairs. The kitchen looks like a tornado came and wreaked havoc. Pots, pans and kitchen utensils caked with who knows what cover every inch of the kitchen counter. The counter isn't even visible. It's disgusting.

"Out here!" Lucas voice calls through the screen door to the patio.

"I'm not cleaning any of this up," Bren mumbles, earning a sleepy nod of agreement from Syd, who's been napping the last hour.

"They couldn't even pay me to help," Syd declares.

My eyes widen, stunned and in awe as I walk out the patio. My mouth waters, and it has nothing to do with the food. All of the guys—even Keith and Brooks—stand in a row in front of the table shirtless, wearing nothing but aprons and swim trunks. The aprons are an array of patterns, ranging from "Kiss the Chef" to floral patterns to something that looks to be Disney related.

"I take it back. If they do some type of Magic Mike dance, I'll help clean the kitchen," Syd whispers, causing me to let out an obnoxious laugh, complete with a snort.

"I didn't know that this dinner came with a show," Bren teases, pulling out her phone. She is always ready to capture the content. The fans are going to eat this up.

"We always aim to entertain," Ryder responds with a wink to Bren. The new kid is coming on strong. He fits right in. "Have a seat, ladies. Keith will lead you through the tasting."

"I like a man who takes charge," Libby murmurs.

"Yeah, Lib, does Blaine take charge?" Syd retorts. Libby gives her a menacing glare that is so ice cold even a quick chill runs through me from witnessing it.

Keith hands us all three different note cards to score each dish based on presentation, taste, creativity, and use of the secret ingredient, dried apricots.

"Sadly, you can't include the actual presentation of the chef in your scores," Tyler says as he waves a hand down his body. "The chefs must remain secret."

With a very evident eye roll, Keith instructs us which dish to taste first. It appears to be chicken and mashed potatoes. Bren cuts into the chicken and I gape at the pink slimy center she reveals.

"I am not eating that," Bren protests. "This entrée gets a zero. It's not edible."

"I told you we needed to cook it longer!" Blake hisses to Harlan.

"We can try the potatoes!" I chime in, trying to find the positive in the grotesque situation. Squeezing my eyes shut, I reluctantly take the smallest bite possible of the mashed potatoes. Not bad. They are garlicky and smooth. I take another bite, reassuring the girls before they take a taste as well.

"Mmm, tasty!" Bren declares, jotting down some notes on her scorecard as the girls whisper their feedback to each other.

"Next dish!" Keith places another chicken dish in front of us with broccoli. This one appears to be thoroughly cooked with a crisp outside bordering more on burnt than browned. As I cut into the chicken, it's a little rubbery, but I would take overcooked chicken over food poisoning any day.

The sweetness delights my tastebuds as I take a bite of broccoli. "Does this broccoli have apricots mixed in?" I ask.

"Yes! It's good, right?" Ryder proclaims. Tyler elbows him, signaling for him to be quiet. We clearly know who the first two dishes belong to, which means Lucas and Blaine have the last one.

"Last dish!" Keith announces when Brooks sets a beautifully plated dish in front of us. There are slices of pork topped with some type of sauce and broccolini. My absolute favorite.

"Wow, that looks like it's from a restaurant," Bren mumbles.

If my tastebuds were delighted by the tangy, sweetness of the broccoli from Tyler and Ryder, then my tastebuds must be in heaven right now. A small moan almost slips from my lips as I take another bite.

"Holy hell," Bren says, putting her hand on her mouth.

"Yep. This wins! No competition," Syd declares.

"What is it? I need it daily. Tell me now," Libby demands, licking her fork clean of the impeccable sauce.

"Pork tenderloin with a peach, apricot glaze," Blaine responds, his eyes locked on Libby as she goes for another bite.

"And broccolini," Lucas chimes in.

"Broccolini is my favorite!" I state, my eyes locking with Lucas, who mouths, "I know" and gives me a wink.

"Of course they win," Tyler complains, the towel that was over his shoulder minutes ago now on the ground.

"Tyler, don't be a sore loser," Bren teases him.

"Your chicken was overcooked, Tyler," I explain, not understanding why Tyler is being so bitter. "But the broccoli was great."

"It's cool. We tried!" Ryder shrugs. "Now, I'm starving."

"I ordered a fuck ton of tacos from a place down the street, they should be here in five minutes," Blaine announces.

"Wow, that was nice of you!" Libby says.

"You can thank my mom. Her credit card paid for it."

"Must be nice to have Mommy get you whatever you want," Tyler mumbles. My mouth thins into a line as I glare at him so sharply it might burn a hole through him. Tyler instantly looks away, avoiding my frustration. What has gotten into him today?

"Thanks, Blaine." Lucas pats him on the back before making his way over to me.

"Where did you learn to cook like that, mysterious boyfriend of mine?" I ask Lucas.

"It was all Blaine," he responds, "minus the broccolini, of course."

"Of course," I laugh. "Blaine, you really outdid yourself."

He shrugs. "I spent a lot of time cooking with my grandma growing up."

"Really? That's surprising," Libby flirtatiously mocks him, bumping her shoulder against him.

Blaine flips his hat so it's facing backward. "Not really . . . I pretty much lived with her every summer. She's southern and loves to cook."

Before Libby or I can respond, Blaine says, "Hey, Ryder, come help me get the tacos."

Blaine Mitchell not only is a phenomenal cook, but he learned how to cook because of his sweet, southern grandma? Surprising doesn't even begin to cover that new information.

Chapter Eleven

Lucas

Disliking Blaine right off the bat when he joined the team was probably wrong of me. I never took the chance to get to know him, but in the last few hours, I've learned more about Blaine Mitchell than I have in the last three years.

I'm pretty sure he grew up opposite to how I did. Blaine spent his summers with his grandma growing up. He didn't say it, but I'm assuming he was always with her to avoid his parent's divorce.

When he brought up his parents, he was short. He changed the topic quickly anytime he mentioned his mom or dad. All I've known is that his mom has money and seemingly gives him whatever he wants. I'm not going to pry, but it seems like there is a lot more than he lets on behind those purse strings.

He's also a damn good cook, which I frankly could use some of his skills. I scored points with Laur by adding broccolini to our meal, but other than cutting shit up and following Blaine's direction, I barely did anything.

While we were in the kitchen, I told him a little bit about my summers here with my family and how we always got Pinto's just down the street at least twice every trip. Blaine ordered tacos from Pinto's, which I mentioned was my favorite spot.

"Thanks again for the tacos, Blaine." I hand him a plate before sitting down next to Laur.

"No problem," Blaine responds, snagging the chair on the other side of Laur.

"What's the plan for tonight?" Ryder asks with his mouth completely full.

"You all are cleaning up that kitchen after we eat," Laur declares, giving Ryder a stern look.

"Right." Ryder boyishly clears his throat, accepting there is no arguing with Laur. "But after that? We've only got one night left after today."

"We never got any shooting practice in with Luc's old equipment," Keith mentions.

Thank God. The game calls to me like the tide under a full moon anytime I take a few days off.

"We should have just done that instead of the stupid cooking thing," Tyler mumbles under this breath.

"Stop being a sore loser, Ty," Libby teases, sticking her tongue out at him.

The damn kitchen takes over an hour to clean between the six of us, solidifying my lack of enthusiasm to do another cooking competition any time soon. We sluggishly wash pots and pans, grunting with discontent.

A loud clash echoes throughout the house as several clean pots and utensils fall to the grease riddled floor.

"You've got to be fucking kidding me." Tyler slams his first on the counter.

"Not a big deal," Keith assures him with a pat on the back. "We'll just give these ones an extra wash."

"Great. Just what I want to do on vacation, wash more dishes." Tyler's nostrils flare. A flash of fury clouds his eyes as if he's about to punch something. Or someone.

Before the cloud turns into a storm, I intervene, "Tyler, go walk it off."

"Whatever you say, Captain." Tyler gives me a mocking salute and walks straight out the open doors to the patio.

What the hell's gotten into him? He's been in a mood all day damn.

As my hands wrap around my old hockey stick, a much-needed calm relief washes over me. Hockey has been my escape my entire life. It's been the one thing I can always rely on to clear my head and set me straight. The pressure of this year might be starting to change that, but not today.

A centering air fills my lungs. On the exhale, my blade scrapes the concrete and connects with the ball, sending it to the back of the net before Keith can move an inch. Keith blocks my next two shots, but my final six shots mimic the first. Sweet victory!

"Damn it," Keith mutters under his breath.

"Nice, Captain Hotshot." Laur beams at me from across the driveaway. A cocky smile starts to dance across my face, but I bite my bottom lip to keep it at bay and remain humble.

"Blaine, you're up. King, you're on deck," I call as I saunter toward Laur and the girls.

"I bet you fifty bucks Ryder sinks every puck," Sydney not so subtly whispers to Libby.

"Technically, it's a ball not a puck, Syd," Libby corrects her friend. In boxes with plenty of equipment from my teenage years playing with my cousins, I found some old street hockey balls perfect for shooting around on the driveway.

"Whatever, Lib," Sydney snaps back. The drama in her eyeroll could rival the sassiest of Bren's signature looks—I'm sure of it. "Are you taking the bet or not?"

"Fine." Libby extends her hand to Sydney, and they shake on their bet.

"Didn't know you were placing bets on my team," I comment, curious how many times over this trip a bet has been placed.

Sydney blushes, and Libby lets out a nervous laugh, "This is the first one we've made all summer, I swear!"

"We've got to keep it interesting somehow," Sydney mumbles, earning a few giggles from Bren and Laur.

"Bored?" I ask, cocking an eyebrow at Laur.

"With you? Never," Laur responds, moving next to my side and interlacing her finger with mine. "But if I was a betting woman, I would put all my money on you, Lucas."

"Get a room," Bren teases. Sydney makes an audible gagging noise of disgust.

In a low growl, I whisper into Laur's ear, "Oh we will definitely be getting a room later."

My sultry comment earns me a playful hit to the chest as Laur's cheeks turn a deep scarlet. Slowly pulling her into me, I plant a delicate kiss on her neck and wrap my arms tightly around her body. My only desire is to be with her however I can be.

My eyes instinctively close as I inhale Laur's sweet perfume, losing myself in the comfort of being with her. Hockey is my first love and my first escape, but just being around Laur challenges its place—always pushing for a tie instead of settling for being a close second.

"Holy shit." Laur's voice pulls me out of my trance.

"I should have put my money on your boyfriend, Libby," Sydney huffs in surprise.

"Shut up, Syd. He's not my boyfriend," Libby snorts, folding her arms.

While I daydreamed, Blaine Mitchell made eight shots in a row. He looks like the shots didn't even faze him. Keith is a damn good goalie—one of the top ranked in NCAA Division I ice hockey. My jaw drops as Blaine snipes his last shot.

"Yeah, definitely should have bet on Libby's boyfriend," Sydney stutters, stunned at what just happened.

"B MAN! You buried that beauty. Fucking nice!" Ryder claps Blaine on the back in congratulations.

"Don't call me that," Blaine snaps, disgust in his voice. He clenches his fist, ready to take off Ryder's head. *What the fuck.* I guess Blaine is back to his normal douchebag antics. As quickly as possible, I start to move to intervene and protect Ryder from being decked in his pretty face. But something stops me in my tracks. Blaine's shoulders subtly rising and falling slowly like he is trying to calm himself down.

Slowly shaking his head as if to clear it, Blaine sighs loudly and mutters, "Sorry, King." Blaine takes a sharp inhale again before continuing "Just. *Don't* call me that. *Capiche?*"

My eyes widen in disbelief. Blaine kept his cool somehow. Maybe he really is turning over a new, unexpected leaf.

Seemingly unfazed by Blaine's reaction, Ryder gives a slight nod. "Yeah, Mitch, *capiche.*"

Blaine, apparently now going by Mitch, pats Ryder on the back. "Thanks. You're up, Prodigy. Show us what you're made of."

Chuckling, Ryder says, "Mitch, I won't lie to you. I'm a little rusty on the street so don't get your hopes up too high."

He weeds through the old hockey sticks. All the sticks are ancient and shitty, but he tests his grip on each one before settling on one and standing in front of the net.

After tapping the bottom of each shoe with the blade of the stick, Ryder turns to his left and spits on the ground then narrows his eyes at the goal. Air fills my lungs as I hold my breath waiting for him to take his first shot. He turns to spit to his right before sending the ball forward and burying it in the back of the net. His next three shots follow suit, beautifully popping each one in. Unfortunately, the rest don't make it in.

"You're a damn skilled tendy, Keith," Ryder approaches the goalie to shake his hand unfazed his shots were deflected when most of the boys would be fuming. "A real ice guardian."

"Some prodigy," Tyler mutters only loud enough for me and Blaine to hear.

"Shake off your attitude, Barret. This is just for fun." Blaine exhales in irritation.

"What was that, Mitchell? Trying to start shit with me?" Tyler demands, his jaw tightening as his body stiffens, fist clenching at his sides, readying himself for what comes next.

"It's good, Barret," Blaine steadily responds, taking a step back.

"Fuck you, Mitchell. Stop with your nice guy act. You aren't fooling anyone, especially Libby," Tyler spits out the last words, seething. "Just come at me already."

Blaine's distressed eyes meet mine as Tyler lunges forward, putting his entire weight behind his punch. Chaos ensues. It takes three guys to hold Tyler back. Sydney's high-pitch screams echo around us, along with some extremely loud profanities from the others.

A few drops of blood stain the pavement, but it isn't from Blaine.

"Got my lip real good, Barret." Ryder barks out a laugh. His hand goes to his mouth. "Nice swing."

Thunderous rage fills me as I realize Tyler, one of the contenders for alternate captain, just punched our newest star player in the face.

Fucking great.

"Fuck. I didn't mean—"

Ryder cuts Tyler off.

"Nah, man, I stepped in. My fault." Ryder pulls his hand away from his mouth. His lip gleams with the sheen of crimson blood. From the looks of it, it's going to swell badly.

"I didn't—" Tyler starts again, his shoulders sagging.

"Barret, next time, I'll be swinging right back, even if it's not meant for me," Ryder jokes. "The season hasn't started, so I can't play this off as a sexy injury just yet."

Tyler's sorrowful eyes avoid my furious stare. "Fucking get him some ice before I decide you need some yourself, Barret." Tyler scurries inside the second I bark out the order.

What is happening? Tyler might get into a mess or two with a girl, but he's not someone who would punch someone on our team over something as trivial as being called out about his bad attitude.

And now, all the negative shit is impacting me too. Even if Tyler deserves to be reprimanded, threatening to punch one of my guys is very out of character for me, especially if it's not someone who typically stirs up issues.

Everyone is acting like a bunch of assholes. This summer better not turn into one of those fucking soap operas my mother loves.

Chapter Twelve

Laur

"What the actual hell are you thinking, Tyler?" My outrage yell mixes with the forceful slam of the sliding door behind me, causing Tyler to flinch.

After Tyler brought an ice for Ryder's face, Bren, Libby, and I quickly coerced him back inside to lecture our dear friend.

"You've been on a different level lately," Bren furrows her brows, "What's gotten into you?"

"Nothing," Tyler huffs out, folding his arms defensively across his chest.

"That's a bold lie." Libby's voice is colder than the glare she sends Tyler from across the room. It's cold enough to turn water into ice.

Tyler's previously defensive arms drop to his side, each fist clenched in aggravation. "Mitchell's been a pain in the ass all day," Tyler retorts harshly. "He was asking for it."

"Are we witnessing the same Blaine Mitchell?" Bren questions him as if she's read my mind. Blaine Mitchell has been a saint since the end of last season.

"He's different around the guys." Tyler's voice is a pitch lower than before. His eyes dart around the room, avoiding eye contact.

"Bullshit, Tyler," Libby calls him out.

"Protecting your not-so-secret lover?" Tyler snarls at Libby, a fire back in his eyes.

My jaw drops at the abrasiveness of Tyler's comment, while Libby's clenches tightly.

Despite the sorrow starting to fill her eyes, she throws each word at Tyler as if it's a dagger aimed for the heart. "Next time don't expect Blaine to be so understanding, or Lucas for that matter." She turns to storm up the stairs only stopping to spit out, "I would have been happy to see Blaine lay you flat on your ass."

"Wow." Bren's tone goes into mama bear mode. "That was a douche move, Tyler. Since when do you treat your friends that way?"

Furiously following Libby, the patio door slams behind Bren.

The walls seemed to cringe at the silence that settles between Tyler and me. His big brown eyes meet mine, pleading for compassion. Even the stillness seems to be begging me to comfort him and fill the quiet void.

"If you are looking for sympathy, you won't get it from me." My voice remains melancholy, despite my irritation and disappointment with him.

"I . . ." Tyler starts, but I instantly cut him off.

"Honestly, Ty, I don't want to hear your excuse." I stare fiercely into his soul, hoping to find some truth behind what's gotten into him, but self-pity seems to be the only thing present in his wide-eyed gaze.

"If you don't stop whatever that is, you're going to make this season," I pause, trying to rein in all the profanities I want to yell at him, "difficult. And not just for yourself. For everyone."

Tyler remains silent, not even acknowledging or agreeing. Throwing my hands up in defeat, I dash inside and upstairs to my room. I release a loud exhausted sigh as I sit on the bed, head in my hands.

Did Nick ever have to deal with this between his players? Did he intervene like Lucas? Nick was loyal and level-headed. I'm sure he stepped in when he needed to.

Laying back on the bed, my heavy eyelids close and I start to drift off. My mind and body both need a break. I thought men were supposed to be low drama, but it seems like I will have to constantly remind myself I'm dealing with a bunch of boys. Boys with massive egos.

A gentle nudge on my arm and a soft delicate kiss on my temple stirs me awake. The most beautiful golden eyes meet my sleepy graze, but no amount of grogginess could stop me from grinning wide at the sight of Lucas when I first wake up.

"Hi, sleeping beauty." Lucas beams, brushing the hair out of my face.

Stretching up, I put my arms around his neck and pull him down so he's laying down next to me. A big, unexpected yawn works its way free.

Laughing, Lucas says, "None of that. I'll stick my finger in your mouth next time!"

Playfully, I let out a dramatic gasp, "You wouldn't dare, Lucas Donato."

"Oh, I would dare." He smirks, bringing his face to meet mine. "Didn't you learn I don't mind being dared or did you already forget our skinny-dipping escapades."

"Maybe I need you to remind me," I coo against his lips.

"Damn it, I knew I should have woken you up thirty minutes ago," he groans, kissing me frantically before springing up off the bed. "But you have ten minutes before we leave for the island themed bar."

My lip pouts in protest, wanting to stay put in bed with Lucas beside me.

"You're the one who said we need to let loose and convinced me to go on this trip!" He swats at my behind playfully and mutters, "Trust me, I miss being walking distance from a rink."

"Fine," I groan, "what am I getting ready for."

"The last night at the beach bar," Lucas responds. "Can't you tell by my attire?" He gestures to his navy short sleeve button down hanging slightly open to show off his delectable muscles paired with his khaki swim trunks.

"Oh yes." I roll my eyes mockingly, "our beach bar attire is vastly different from than what you've been wearing this entire trip."

Slowly, I rise out of bed, letting out another yawn. Before I know what's happening, a finger is shoved into my mouth. I let out a cry of surprise.

"Told you I would do it," Lucas mumbles, a boyish grin plastered across his stubbled face.

Taking a step toward him, I narrow my eyes and threaten, "Next time, I'll bite."

Lucas raises his eyebrows at me, and whispers, "Promise?"

"Get out of here," I squeal, tempted to grab a pillow off the bed and chuck it at him. "It's already been at least two minutes, and you will make me take much longer."

Before he can object, I teasingly shove him towards the door.

Reggae music dances through the salty air, complementing the sound of the waves and competing with the noisy bar, almost packed wall to wall unlike last time.

"THERE!" Blake points across the patio to a group of people gathering their things to leave.

"Move, men!" Tyler commands, seemingly in a lighter mood than when I saw him a few hours ago. Hopefully, his newfound positive attitude stays the entire night.

"Go, go, go!" Blake darts and weaves through tables and people, almost knocking over a waitress, to claim the table for our group. He gives the rest of our group, who slowly make our way over to ensure we don't knock down any staff members, a double thumbs up before shouting, "OVER HERE!"

The goofiness makes me chuckle, and I mutter to Bren, "Did he have a few drinks before this?"

"Oh absolutely," Bren confirms. "Pretty sure everyone but you did."

"Nope, I did not," Tyler chimes in, overhearing us.

"Probably for the best," Bren mumbles, patting him on the shoulder before darting away to the bar before Tyler can dish out a comeback.

"Laur, about earlier," Tyler starts to apologize, his hands sheepishly finding his pockets.

"Let's just enjoy the last night," I quietly reply. My pulse speeds up with the anxiety of having to talk about Tyler's antics. Again. Avoiding him, I quickly turn away to sit down next to Lucas.

Releasing a loud sign, Tyler turns to head to the bar. I meant what I said. I really want to just enjoy the last night we have on the beach. Once we get back to campus, reality will hit. My responsibilities linger in the back of my mind, reminding me they're there like an unread text notification.

Something cold taps my shoulder, shaking me out of my trance.

"Thanks, Bren," I say as she hands me the crisp, cold light beer.

"Cheers to a good last night." She grins, clinking her beer bottle against mine.

"Looks like someone is already having a good night," Lucas mutters.

Before I can ask Lucas what he's talking about, my ears ring with the most obnoxious attempt at flirtatious giggles I have ever heard in my life. My eyes widen at the sight of not one but two girls clinging to Ryder—girls is probably not an accurate way to describe them. They are significantly older than the eighteen year old kid.

"Guess the rumors about Ryder aren't just rumors," Blake mutters.

"That guy's got some mad game," Keith responds. "Those ladies are at least ten years older than him."

"Oh please." Blaine rolls his eyes. "He's got nothing. The boy's an amateur."

Libby stifles a laugh, almost spitting out her umbrella topped mix drink.

"What, you think that's funny?" Blaine's voice carries a teasing tone despite his brows furrowing.

"Yeah, I do," Libby retorts casually.

In one smooth swift motion, Blaine swipes Libby's drink from her.

"Hey! Give me back my drink!" Libby squeals playfully.

With a sly smile, Blaine takes a sip of her drink, "Tell me why you think it's funny, then I will."

"What are you five?" Libby snorts.

"No, but Ryder is," Blaine mumbles, getting a chuckle out of a few of the guys.

"Well, the five-year-old has more game than you," Libby bites back, everyone now laughing at our table. Well, everyone except Blaine.

Blaine raises an eyebrow before loudly slurping down the rest of the drink he swiped from Libby.

"Still got you, didn't I?" He winks playfully. "I'll go get you another drink."

Stunned into silence, no one at our table says anything for more than a beat.

"I'm not going to lie," Keith whispers next to me. "That was some pretty damn impressive game Mitchell just dished out."

Bren turns her head in every direction, catching my attention.

"Has anyone seen, Tyler?" Bren asks, now standing up from her seat to look around the beach bar.

"He went home," Ryder proclaims as he walks up with his new friends.

"What are you talking about?" I question; my mind begins to race with anxious thoughts. Why did he leave? Did he really go home?

"Yeah," Ryder replies, holding one of the woman's hands, while the other drapes herself all over him, vying for his attention. "After his first beer, he tapped my shoulder while I was talking to Jillian and Jackie. Told me he was over it and headed out."

"That's . . ." Bren pauses, her face scrunched in confusion and concern.

"Not like him," I finish.

"No big deal, he probably just needed to blow off some steam," Blake casually explains, like a typical guy not thinking anything is a big deal.

Libby thumbs strike faster than lightning as she quickly taps out a text on her phone, likely to check on Tyler.

Keith pulls his phone out too. "I'll shoot him a text. Anyone want anything from the bar?"

A few "No thanks" and head shakes are the only responses Keith gets.

"I'm sure he's fine." Lucas tries to comfort us with his easy words and pulls me close to his side.

"He just texted me back," Libby sighs with relief. "He said he's back at the house, and he was tired."

"Why does everyone look like something bad just happened," Blaine asks, coming back to the table. "My joke wasn't that terrible." He hands Libby a fresh drink that's twice the size of her previous one.

"Tyler left without telling anyone," Bren complains.

"Technically he told Ryder," Keith corrects Bren, earning him a fierce eyeroll from her.

"So? He's a big kid. He can take care of himself," Blaine states nonchalantly, taking a sip from his beer.

"He's got someone taking care of him," Ryder chimes in, back from the bar insanely fast. And surprisingly solo. It seemed to take Blaine at least three times as long to get a drink.

"Yeah, he's with a lady friend in our pool." Ryder waggles his eyebrows. "Told you he was fine."

"That's a very different text back than I got . . ." Libby utters softly.

"Enough about Tyler," Blaine blurts out. "They have cornhole. Who wants to go play?"

"Who calls it cornhole?" Bren jokes with him as Ryder shouts, "Yes, sirrrrr!" dragging the "r" at the end out longer than necessary.

"I'm from the south," Blaine shrugs.

"Dude, you're from Florida," Blake proclaims, standing up to join them.

"Which is in the south, bro, where we play cornhole." Blaine shakes his head at Blake's clueless comment.

"Fine," Libby groans. "If you stop saying cornhole, I'll grace you with my bag skills."

"Deal," Blaine agrees as a grin quickly stretches from ear to ear. Maybe it's just the alcohol he drank, but he seems very smitten over Libby tonight.

"Let's all go," Bren suggests, eyeing me.

Lucas' eyes meet mine. "Yeah, we'll be there in a minute," Lucas answers for me, reading my mind.

"I'm just worried about Tyler," I start as soon as Lucas and I are alone.

"Blaine's right, he's an adult," Lucas states. "He's the only one other than me that didn't drink before we came out. He's probably just needing some alone time."

Twirling the ends of my hair, I let out a weary sigh.

"I know, you're probably right . . . but,"

"No, we are having fun tonight. No more worrying," Lucas kisses my forehead, "Unless it's about how I'm about to kick your ass at cornhole."

"You don't want to be on my team?!" I shriek back at him, excited to get my mind off Tyler's Irish Goodbye.

Lucas stands up offering me his hand. "No ma'am, you know I love a bet."

Swatting his hand playfully away, I tease him, "Be ready to lose." I quickly dart away from the table calling back to him "Don't worry, babe, I accept Venmo."

"We are going to miss our flight if you guys don't hurry up!" Bren's shout fills the house. To no surprise, the guys rush at the last minute packing their things this morning. None of them packed last night except Lucas. How typical.

When we got back home last night, Tyler and his mystery girl were nowhere to be found. With the chaos of trying to get everyone out the door this morning, I didn't get a chance to try to talk to Tyler alone this morning. The sound of his animated voice giddily gossiping about this year's upcoming NHL draft with Keith can be heard from my seat two rows in front of him. At least he seems to be back to his usual self.

My stomach turns the entire flight home even though there wasn't any turbulence. Anxiety weighs on me knowing Bren's departure date looms and I'm going to be running the show on my own.

On the plus side, my Venmo balance was a little higher than the night before. I'm the bags reigning champion—take that, Lucas Donato!

Chapter Thirteen
Laur

"S UZ!" Bren's buoyant shriek fills our entire house and echoes off the walls with Suz's arrival for one last hurrah.

Jaylin, my hippie, weed-loving roommate, who happens to be Suz's girlfriend, takes Suz' bag up to her room as the rest of us head to the living room. Plopping aimlessly down on the couch, my mind floats elsewhere. The first-round interviews start tomorrow. Thankfully they're virtual, which will give me some practice before in-person rounds start.

A pillow soars through the air, softly hitting my shoulder, breaking me out of my stress-induced trance.

"Earth to Laur!" Bren snaps at me. "Did you order the pizza?"

"I've been craving Tailgate's buttery crust since I left," Suz comments, licking her lips.

Calling from the stairs, Jaylin confirms she's already ordered. "Libby graciously offered to pick it up on her way over too!"

"Speaking of Libby . . . are you ready for some new tea, Suz? It's piping hot." Bren beams with bubbly delight, practically bouncing on the couch, eager to share.

"Let me grab the wine first!" Suz exclaims, clapping her hands, "God forbid we share any gossip without a drink in hand!"

Ding-dong.

Thunderous steps rush down the stairs as Jaylin shouts, "I got it!" while answering the door. The delicious smell of pizza fills the living room as Libby enters the house.

"Oh marvelous, she can spill her own tea," Bren mutters, her guilty eyes meeting mine. She knows I loathe being involved in gossip. Do I like to hear it? Absolutely, what female doesn't? I try not to share what's not mine to tell, but apparently I have a big mouth today.

Wine glasses clink in Suz's hands as she carries in two bottles of cheap red wine and three glasses, Jaylin behind her with plates and the other two glasses, followed by Libby with our dinner.

"I'm starved," Suz proclaims, setting down the wine on the coffee table and immediately opening the giant pizza box as soon as Libby puts it down next to the wine.

"And thirsty apparently," Jaylin remarks, opening one of the screw top bottles of wine. "Are you expecting more people than just the five of us?"

"Well, I didn't want to have to move and miss the scandalous scoop of what's going on with Libby," Suz declares, wincing as she takes a bite of the still steaming pizza.

Through pursed lips, Libby asks what in the hell Suz is talking about.

Silence fills the room, no one willingly brave enough to break it. Without thinking, I hold my breath automatically, waiting for the drama to ensue as soon as a word is uttered.

"I didn't tell her anything!" Guilt laces Bren's voice. To be honest, I'm not sure I've seen my cousin stay quiet this long my entire life.

Libby's eyes narrow, harshly glaring at Bren as if trying to pull an admission out of her.

After guzzling her wine, Bren confesses, "I just told her there were some spicy rumors!"

With delight sparkling in her eye, Suz chimes in, "Spicy? You did not tell me anything about it being spicy. Now, I'm sure we need the third bottle of wine."

Libby holds up her empty glass for Suz to fill, taking a big, sloppy sip and wiping the remnants of the shitty wine off her lips before letting out a big sigh and starting to explain. "I guess I kind of have a thing with Blaine Mitchell."

A tiny gasp rises from Suz. "Well good thing I didn't just take a sip of wine." She nervously laughs. "I would have spit it all over the cream-colored carpet."

Bren narrows her eyes at Libby, questioning her, "What do you mean kind of? It's a definite thing. I've seen it. Laur has too!"

My voice sharp and defensive, I cut in, "Don't bring me into this. I'm just here to eat pizza, and spend time with my favorite people before another one of them leaves me."

Jaylin, usually just a bystander in the Suz and Bren Gossip Brigade, joins in on questioning Libby. "You know he's an asshole, right? I mean you have to know you've been around him."

Libby releases a big sigh, as if the question alone exhausts her to her very core. "He can be, but he isn't always."

Ever the gossip, Bren interjects, "Actually Tyler has been more of one lately."

Suz dramatically puts a hand to her heart, as if the shock of this news has wounded her. "Wait what? I leave campus for a few months and everything changes."

Not ready to start thinking about Tyler's antics again, I blurt out, "Blaine is less of a douche, Tyler is more of a douche. Ryder King is a hot commodity. Not everything has changed."

Suz claps her hands enthusiastically, practically jumping off the couch to hear more. "Oh I was waiting for Ryder to come up! But now I'm more interested in hearing about Blaine." Suz cocks her head at Libby. "Not to be rude, but . . ." Her lashes lower, her eyes becoming mere slits, as if trying to understand Libby's soul. "Why Blaine?"

Bren inserts herself. "He still has a bad reputation, even if he has been less, "she pauses searching for the right word. "*Blaine* the last month or two."

"I get it. You think I like chasing red flags," Libby fiercely fires back, her face turning red with frustration.

My hands grow clammy from this conversation. I set my wine glass down, worried it will slip out of my grasp.

"You're putting words in my mouth," Bren retorts. "I just want you to be happy."

Libby drains her wine glass in a few quick slurps, clearly ready to be done with this conversation. "I'm happy with how things are right now." Without asking, she picks up my full glass and starts to drain that one too. "Not everyone needs the perfect long-distance relationship like you and Liam have."

Bren snorts. "Our relationship is far from perfect."

Libby sets my finished wine glass down, and grabs another slice of pizza, taking a big bite. With her mouth full she practically spits out the words, "Oh please."

Tears pull in the corner of Bren's eyes as her face transforms, her lips quivering and her expression full of agony. "I haven't talked to him in an entire week okay. Happy? It's not perfect." Bren's voice is barely a whisper.

My heart sinks to my stomach at her confession. I had no idea Bren was struggling with Liam. I wish she told me. Softly I assure her, "Bren no one is happy that you're upset, don't be silly. We love you."

Head nodding, Libby agrees adding, "We are always here for you, why didn't you say anything?"

A few tears stream from Bren's eyes, her voice quiet and quivering when she says, "What am I supposed to say?" She grabs a napkin, loudly blowing her knows. "Suz already left me. I have to leave you guys, which breaks my heart, and my boyfriend is too busy living out his dream to talk to me, but I shouldn't be sad. I get to start my literal dream job next week."

The tears steadily flow down Bren's round cheeks. She sniffles, grabbing another napkin to use as a tissue.

Moving to be closer to her on the couch, I pull my cousin into a side hug, wishing I could ease her pain. "Oh, Brennie Bean, I'm so sorry. It's a lot of change, but you'll get through it. We all will."

Suz moves to fill everyone's empty wine glasses before adding, "I know I don't share much about it but you know I'm a private person. I'm working on being okay with everything that's changed after graduation too."

Looking around the room at each of us, Bren's gaze falls on me. "Please stop looking at me like I'm Bambi after the mom dies."

Suz hands Bren a now full to the brim wine glass. "I'm always just a phone call away."

"Do you want to go out tonight?" Libby asks. "Get your mind off things and let loose?"

Bren reluctantly shakes her head. "No, I don't want to share my best friends with the rest of the world on my last night." Her eyes meet mine as she sips her wine. "Is that okay?"

I squeeze her to my side again. "Whatever you need, Brennie Bean."

A heavy sigh escapes Bren as she nuzzles into my side and rests her head on my shoulder, setting her full wine glass on the side table. "Better wine. The kind that comes with a real cork in it next time."

Chapter Fourteen

Laur

My heart rate slows and a lump forms in the back of my throat as Bren and I carry the last of her boxes down the stairs of our house. By some miracle, my eyes are still dry. It hasn't hit me that she's really leaving.

While Bren instructs her moving crew, which just consists of some of the hockey players, I do one last sweep of her room to make sure she hasn't missed anything. The room is bare. No bed, no dresser. There's even a blank space on her wall where just hours ago a picture of us and one of her and Liam hung. Not a single thing is left in her closet.

The floodgates open, and tears stream down my face. My heart is as empty as the room is.

"Oh, babe, come here." Lucas walks into the room and pulls me into a hug. "It's going to be okay."

"I know," I sob into his chest, trying to avoid leaving mascara stains on his t-shirt. "But I'm going to miss her."

"Me too," he replies, giving me a tight squeeze. "The guys and I are going to leave so you can say bye to Bren."

My head nods against his chest, not ready to let him go yet.

"Oh, before I forget, Suz left this note for you." Lucas pulls away, handing me an envelope.

For my heart's sake, I'm thankful Suz left at the crack of dawn. My puffy red eyes can't possibly handle more tears right now.

"I'll text you when we are done with interviews tonight." My voice shakes, sadness still clouding my vision.

After heading downstairs, I hug Lucas one more time before he leaves. I turn to Bren standing outside her car, ready to say goodbye.

My sobs start again and sorrow slowly rolls down my face. Bren pulls me to her in an embrace that instantly tightens. I don't want to let her go.

"I love you, but you are suffocating me like a boa constrictor," Bren mutters through clenched teeth.

Hesitantly, I break our embrace, wiping the tears from my eyes.

Bren smiles at me through her tears. "I'll only be a few hours away, and you can call me any time you need me."

"Promise you'll come visit?" My voice cracks on the last word.

"Of course," Bren assures me, pulling me into another tight hug.

"And I can call you after the interviews today?"

"Of course," Bren assures me again. "But you won't need me. You're going to be amazing, Laur."

Climbing into her car, she blows me a kiss goodbye and leaves the driveaway of the house we've shared for the last year.

Being at West without Nick was difficult for me, but now not having Bren on campus will feel lonelier than ever. What am I going to do?

Opening the note Suz left for me, a small smile breaks through my tears.

Laur,

Remember when we pretty much hated each other? Now look at us—best friends. You can get through anything. Bren is just a short drive and a phone call away. I might be a long flight away, but I'm always a phone call away too.

When you've finished interviews, send me an email. I want to partner with you on some content for before the season starts on the Wyverns and on Ryder King. He's been a hot topic at USA Hockey

Magazine. Think you could interview him for me to go along with an article I'm writing about him? Let me know!

The Wyverns PR team is in the best hands it can possibly be in.

Smile. You've got this.

xx,

Suz

P. S. Keep any new blondes away from Jaylin for me ;)

P.P.S. Remember you still have Luc, Tyler, and Libby—you aren't alone.

Suz is right. I'm not alone. I've got an amazing support system here and one I can call or text any time I need them.

Taking a deep calming breath, I head into the house to make some coffee and prepare for the first round of interviews.

My shoulders relax, feeling like a weight has lifted from them after completing the first round of PR and marketing candidate interviews. Somehow, it went as smooth as possible. I'm already ready for round two.

My stress has eased, but I could still use something after the long, emotional day. I quickly text Libby to see if she can meet at Hae's for a quick drink and debrief.

"Thank goodness you're still here and leading the interviews," Libby slides into the faux leather booth, "Kat and I would be lost without you."

"I doubt that," I laugh but wonder if Kat would be the lead as the only senior left if I never joined. Kat is incredibly sweet and she's great at taking direction but sometimes struggles giving it. Libby is a born leader, but she might be the least organized person I've ever met.

The second we place a drink order the waitress, Libby throws question after question my way. "So, who's your top contender? Is it that girl Lena that had soccer team experience? How did Lena interview? Do you think it'll be easy to compile your file list in person?"

A giggle slips past my lips. "I appreciate the enthusiasm, Lib, but take a breath." I lift my bottle to my mouth and take a sip of my drink. The cool, refreshing light beer trickles down my throat. It's exactly what I need. "Actually, Lena wasn't my favorite. A girl named Raven was."

Chapter Fifteen
Lucas

The sound of my skates scrapping against the ice calms me. I started coming back to the rink almost daily since we got back from the beach, hungry to feel the sense of ease that only the rink can give me.

Practice finally starts again today. From the videos I've seen before they got extended offers, our new players have some work to do, except for Ryder King.

A blur of motion, Ryder quickly speeds across the ice, beating some of the fastest juniors and seniors on the team during full ice sprints. He reminds me of myself when I was a freshman, confident and at home on the ice.

My eyes widen larger than pucks watching his remarkable stick-handling. Moving through the cones with the grace of wind over glass, Ryder dances down the ice. His turns are tight. His hands are quick. He doesn't miss a beat.

At the blow of a whistle, Assistant Coach Parrish divides us up to scrimmage so the coaching staff can get an idea of where the team is at, where strengths are, where improvements need to be made.

For once in my life, I don't want to be on the ice; I want to sit out so I can observe the players and solidify my choices for alternate captain. Instead, my eyes follow several of the players while I'm on the bench.

To no surprise, Keith stops ninety-nine percent of shots fired at him, continuing to be one of the best goalies I've seen in college hockey.

Each pass from Blake Hursh is crisp and strong, setting up his linemates to shoot flawlessly.

Silas Harlan could be a good contender for an alternate captain. He directs and encourages like a leader on the ice. He defends the net like a mama bear protecting her cub.

My jaw almost drops watching Blaine Mitchell flow across the rink like water—almost as smooth as Ryder. His game has vastly improved. Is his shift in attitude as real as his new skills on the ice?

One thing's for sure, Ryder and Blaine vibe off of each other really damn well. They manage a hot breakaway together during the scrimmage and sneak one in past our backup goalie, Jenson.

"Holy shit." Blake pulls me aside after practice before we headed into the locker room. "Ryder might be better than Nick Bellinger."

That is a bold statement. But there is no doubt in my mind that with Ryder on the team, we have a good shot at making it to the championships this year.

"Hey, Ryder," Keith shouts as we enter the locker room. "Really fucking good job."

"Thanks, Tendie," Ryder calls back with a wide grin across his face. "The Wyverns are ready to kick ass this season!"

Ryder doesn't need his ego stroked, but he gets compliments from just about everyone in the locker room.

"Great practice today, guys." I pull the attention away from him. "But we've got a long way to go to get to that championship this season."

The guys' faces fall at my seriousness, smiles and locker-room jesting seizing.

"But if anyone can do it, it's this fucking team," I bellow, lifting the mood back up. Cheers and chants of excitement erupt around the locker room.

"Donato," Coach demands, walking into the locker room. "Come see me in my office once you've finished up."

A hushed "*Ooooo*" ripples around the locker room.

"Oh please," Blaine says, throwing a towel in my direction. "We know he's not in trouble."

"The world would have to end if he was," Harlan chimes in, chuckling.

"Speaking of the world ending, how's Libby," Ryder teases Blaine.

Blaine cocks an eyebrow at him. "What's she have to do with the world ending?"

A boyish grin starts across Ryder's face. "Because you have a girlfriend. From what I've heard about you, that means the world is ending."

"No one said anything about a girlfriend," Blaine chirps back.

Ryder's sly smile now stretches from ear to ear. "Fuck yeah. Come be my wingman tonight."

Looks like Ryder King is going to give Blaine Mitchell a run for his money as the biggest playboy on the hockey team.

Before I hear something I don't want to hear about Libby, I head down the hall to Coach's office.

"Come in, Donato." Coach Andres gestures for me to close the door behind me.

"I know we've only had one real practice, but I wanted to get your thoughts on this season."

"Honestly?" My eyes meet Coach's. "I think we have a shot at winning the championship. With the new players, Ryder King being elite, and how much Blaine and Harlan have improved, I think we have a good chance of going all the way."

"Keep pushing them, Luc," Coach Andres states, excitement shining in his eyes. "If today is any indication of how the season can go, I think we've got a damn good shot too."

Running my fingers through my hair, my heart pounds knowing how much will be on me this season.

"What are your thoughts on alternate captains?" Coach asks. I knew this was coming, but I'm not ready to give him my suggestions yet.

"I want more time to observe the guys during practice," I sheepishly reply. I know the decision isn't mine alone, but I want to make sure I don't regret who I suggest.

"Two weeks. Otherwise, the coaching staff will make the decision without your recommendations," Coach says sternly.

"Yes, sir." I nod and get up to leave.

"Hey, Lucas," Coach calls to me, causing me to pause before opening the door.

"You've got a lot riding on this season, kid." Coach Andres folds his hands over his stomach. "But don't forget why you started the game in the first place."

Chapter Sixteen

Laur

My heart beats loudly in my ears. This time with more thrill than nerves to finish the second round of interviews, even though part of my excitement is definitely Libby finally being all moved in. Every time I walk past Bren's empty room my heart sinks. Having Libby there will lift some of the sadness out of my heart to see the room full again, especially when my best friend on campus lives down the hall from me.

I already finished the first half of the second round of virtual interviews yesterday before in person interviews happen—if they can make it to in person. Truthfully, I'm debating pushing all final interviews to virtual with the larger team instead of in person. Some candidates might live too far, and we did get a late start on interviewing. I don't want to waste anyone's time; we only have five open spots.

The final interviews are for the other leads, Libby and Kat, who is the only other senior on the team but not close with our friend group, to flag any issues they see, so my mind will be mostly set on who I want to join the program by then.

To have the most positive end to the sessions, I chose to end interviews with the two candidates that I think have the most potential, Lena and Raven. There is no doubt in my mind that they both will get one of the five spots we have open.

Lena's interviews went flawlessly. She was bouncing with glee her entire interview, reminding me of Bren's bubbly mannerisms. She is an absolute yes. Truthfully, I see her being the lead of the program when she's a senior.

Raven I am on the fence about. She has an extensive background in the fashion world. I'm impressed by the number of events she's been a part of, especially so young. She's supported over ten different charity fundraisers, galas, and auctions but it's not clear to me why she wants to work with a hockey team.

Clearing my throat, I immediately inquire about this at the start of her next interview. I need to know why she thinks working for a sports team would be the right fit for her and why she applied to this specific program.

"Tell me why you want to work with a hockey team."

Her eyes go distant as if she is no longer mentally in our virtual interview. "I have a family tie to the fashion industry," Raven explains, her voice quieting. "It's really helped me get my foot in the door."

After a beat she continues, still not fully present. "But I want something different." She twirls her finger around her blonde locks and shakes her head, which seems to bring her back into the present. "I think my experience with the charity events will translate very well." Her voice grows louder with confidence.

Before I can ask her to elaborate, she continues. *Good.* She knows she needs to provide more details.

"I am most excited for the opportunity to help drive ticket sales and raise money for the team's charity focus for the year. I have a lot of ideas on events outside of games as well as events inside of games. I'll share an example." She pauses, taking a breath. "A picnic basket auction, which would be a less vulgar way of auctioning off the players."

My chin perks up listening to her clever idea. Before I joined the team, there was an issue with someone's stepmom and a player getting frisky when she won the auction for that player.

Elaborating on her idea, Raven explains, "Each player would create their own basket filled with food, drinks, dessert, and some type of activity they love. It could range from crossword puzzles to a board game to binoculars to bird watch."

My heart slows after skipping a beat hearing binoculars at first, thankful she explained it was for bird watching. This must be what others feel like when I mention my brother's little black book. It's harmless and insightful with hockey team and player insights galore.

Raven's voice speeds up with enthusiasm. "People would bid on the baskets, not knowing which player created them. We could even have some type of prize if someone guesses each basket correctly to the player on the team—it would be difficult but people love to win hard things."

She drums her finger on her chin, thinking. "There could be an entry fee to guess, maybe some type of raffle to support the charity." She drums her finger on her chin. "Then people would also bid for the baskets so it's two-fold, and we could raise even more money."

My mind races, plotting out the concept. This could be a way to ensure its public facing, and people would be bidding on mystery baskets so technically wouldn't know which player made which basket. Knowing the players, they would definitely need some support coming up with ideas, but luckily, that's right in my team's wheelhouse.

The guessing component as a raffle to raise probably double the amount of money? It's truly remarkable. It's evident she's damn good at charity events.

"Great example! I have one final question for you," I tell Raven, my voice dripping with eagerness. Our interview has already gone over the hour I had planned, but I'm determined to hear more of her ideas around games. "Can you give me an example of a social media post or campaign you would create prior to game day to grow attendance?"

"Can I ask some questions?" Raven replies, poised and calm under the pressure.

"Of course," I respond, interested to hear her questions.

"Who are we playing? What day of the week is the game? Do we have any special or unique marketing opportunities for the game?"

Each question she asks is intuitive. Raven puts a lot of detailed thought into every answer she's given me, except I realize she never gave detail on why sports marketing. Why is she so aloof about that? Libby or Kat will have to re-ask during her final interview.

"Great questions." I clasp my hands together. "Assume we are playing one of our main rivals. It's a Friday game. Any marketing opportunities, swag, whatever you can think of are fair game."

A bright grin bursts across her face. "Perfect! I would focus on the rivalry and create a campaign around the rivalry. I'd maybe call it the rivalry rampage." She pauses, thinking for a moment before continuing. "Scratch that I'm not sure what I would call it yet."

"Let's assume this opponent is someone we typically win against. Outside the arena, there would be a car with the opponent's logo on it. The car would be donated from a local junk yard, already beat up but free to save on costs."

My eyes widen with delight. I like where she is headed.

"People would be able to purchase a ticket. There could even be different tiers. You would place a bet on how much you think we will win by, which would enter them into the rivalry bet," She giggles. "I'm still workshopping the name. But people could spray paint their bets on the car. We could also hit the car with a hockey stick and charge per hit, but from a safety perspective I'm not sure that would fly," she whispers the last part to herself.

Thinking for a minute, I finally reply, "I'm not sure of logistics, but let's just say we can do it for the sake of this hypothetical scenario." What I don't add is how it would need to be an expensive stick with a high flex rating . . . The old sticks the hockey department has wouldn't work and we would not have a budget for endless new sticks.

A sheepish smile spreads across Raven's face. "In that case, each person can pay for up to five hits, pay per ticket. Half the proceeds go to the charity and the other half goes to the winner, who is determined based on the best they placed. We are winning this hypothetical game."

Pride fills my eyes, but I need to try to stump her. "I think this would draw a lot of attention. How would you handle people making the same bet? How would the winner be determined if over fifty people had the same exact score for the game?"

Tapping her finger on her chin, she slowly begins, "It's a raffle, so everyone that guesses correctly would be entered—up to five times, each time you purchase a ticket to hit the car with the hockey stick you get an entry. If you guess correctly, then your tickets go into the raffle."

Boom. She nailed it, this makes up for her strange response to the hockey question. Before I can ask any follow up questions, she jumps back in.

"There would be posts on social media, email marketing, posters around campus. I would love to do a fake promo video with the guys shirtless and hitting the car. Maybe a different car though." Excitement dances in Raven's eyes. "This would be so fun!"

A small, satisfied smile creeps onto my face, I cough trying to keep it from Raven's view.

"Thank you for putting so much intention into your well-crafted responses. I will be in touch in the next few days regarding next steps. Do you have any more questions for me before we end?" I ask, still trying to hide my smile and remain natural.

"I just wanted to confirm—the next steps are the last round, correct?" Raven inquires, her voice slightly shaky.

"Yes. They will be the final interviews. However, I think they will still be virtual for the sake of time," I inform her, "I'll be in touch shortly. Thanks so much for your time."

"Thank you for the time and consideration, Lauren. Have a great day!" Raven says chirpily, the confidence back in her voice.

"You too," I reply, exiting the video call.

Something about Raven feels familiar, but I can't put my finger on it.

Chapter Seventeen
Laur

Walking into my bedroom, I feel infinitely lighter, like a twenty-pound weight has been lifted off of me. Not only did I get approval from the professor lead of the program to formally shift the in-person interviews to virtual, but Bren's old room is no longer empty, causing me heartache.

Looking at the photo of Nick and me on my side table, tears sting my eyes as I whisper, "You'd be so proud of me, big brother. Thank you for forcing me into this program." A small chuckle slips out, thinking about how he truly did force me by applying on my behalf. But I will always be grateful. It brought me to West. It brought me to start healing after his loss and after an abusive relationship. It brought me Lucas.

Wiping a stray fallen tear from my eye, I breathe in deeply. The sound of the front door opening, pulling me out of my trance.

"I'm home!" Libby screeches, coming up the stairs and into her new decorated room.

Since Libby took over, the room has morphed from Bren's bright pink to purple. I wonder if it will transition to blue after Libby, it only seems fitting.

Bursting into my room, she declares, "Our home is officially the same home!"

"I know!" I respond as enthusiastically as I can, thoughts of Nick still heavy on my soul.

"You okay?" Libby asks, concern paints her face.

"I'm okay," I reply. "Just a lot going on this week, but thankfully I get a break today."

"Yes! You deserve a break." Libby practically leaps onto my bed, sitting next to me. "Can we celebrate taking the next step in our friendship?"

Cocking an eyebrow at her in confusion, she reads the confusion on my face. "From best friends to roommates, obviously," Libby explains.

"Ah, right. Of course, what did you have in mind?" I ask, but I already know her obvious answer is the only bar we go to. "Hae's?"

"I was thinking something different." Libby has a wicked grin on her face. "What about Howdy's?"

"The line dancing bar?" My face twists in confusion once more. We've never gone there. Hae's is our spot.

"New beginnings, new spot." Libby shrugs casually.

A laugh bursts out of me. "If it's just the girls. Good luck getting the guys to go to a line dancing bar."

Libby dramatically rolls her eyes, "There's alcohol and girls in daisy dukes, they'll be more than fine." She pulls out her phone, a small smile spreading on her face. "Tyler just agreed, so I'm sure more of the guys will come."

"Cool, I'll tell Lucas we'll meet them there." A mischievous grin slides across my face thinking about Lucas attempting to line dance. Tonight is going to be very entertaining.

The sound of boots stomping blends perfectly with the blaring country music as we enter the bar. Our hockey players stick out like sore thumbs amongst the cowboy hats. My eyes widen taking in that every guy from our typical group joined—even Blaine.

Walking up to Lucas, he instantly hands me my favorite light beer from the bucket on the table.

"Thanks." A grin overtakes my face. Lucas always proves time and time again that chivalry is, in fact, not dead. "Where's your cowboy hat, Captain?"

"Damn." He smiles back. "I knew I was forgetting something."

"Hey, Lib." Blaine warmly greets Libby. Her eyes trail him up and down, but she turns towards the rest of the group, not responding to him.

"Did you know this place used to be called *Second Cousins?*" Blaine tries to get Libby's attention again but gets no response.

Ryder chimes in with a loud snicker. "That's hilarious."

I take a sip of my beer, then mutter, "Good thing they changed the name."

"They should have kept it," Ryder replies. "It could make for a good story."

Before Ryder can elaborate, Libby breaks her silence. "Blaine," she snaps, "why the hell would you wear sandals to a line dancing bar?"

Lucas chuckles, shaking his head baffled. "You're going to stub a toe."

"See, dude, I told you," Ryder says, swatting Blaine on the arm. "You don't wear sandals to a bar where you're supposed to spend half the night stomping on the ground."

Blaine shrugs. "Tyler's wearing them too. Why am I being bullied?"

Libby dramatically rolls her eyes. "Bullied? Yeah, right."

"Oh well, I didn't want to dance anyways," Tyler confesses.

Sydney calls him out. "You both wore them on purpose so you wouldn't have to dance."

Shamelessly pointing finger guns at her, Blaine winks.

Libby crosses her arms. Disdain coats her every word when she says, "We are supposed to be celebrating and having fun."

"Lighten up, Lib." Sydney throws an arm around her. "We just got here."

Blaine raises an eyebrow at Libby, who still has her arms still crossed. "I can still have fun in my sandals."

"Let's go get a drink, Syd," Libby huffs. "I need something stronger than beer."

"What's her deal?" Tyler asks me the second Libby is out of earshot.

Shaking my head, I reply, "I have no idea."

Tyler turns his gaze to Blaine.

"Don't look at me, man." Blaine throws his hands up in innocence. "This is the first time I've talked to her today."

"Dramaaaaa," Ryder belts in a sing-songy voice, "I'm going to put my fake ID to good use. Be back in a few."

My brows furrow. Libby's relationship with Blaine is hard to follow. I assumed she was seeing him after their time at the beach . . . She didn't mention anything about them ending things.

Chapter Eighteen
Lucas

The girls leave their drinks at the high top table with us and go out to the dance floor, where drinks of any kind are not allowed. Libby left the table with a toss of her hair and not a backward glance at Blaine.

Keith and Tyler disappeared, probably to the bar or to talk with some other friends that are here tonight. I knew none of the guys would have any desire to actually dance, but at least it's an excuse for a fun night out.

"At least there are a lot of attractive girls here," Ryder remarks to no one in particular. Turning to Blaine, he says, "If you and Libby called it quits, we have plenty of options."

Blaine clenches his drink tightly. "Who said anything about calling it quits?"

"Sorry, B-Man." Ryder clinks his beer bottle to Blaine's, "I just assumed because she seemed pissed."

Unballing his fist, Blaine sighs. "I don't know what her problem is." He takes a swig of his drink.

Needing to find a way to avoid being part of this conversation, I push away from the table. "I'm going to go find my girlfriend." I turn to go to the dance floor.

Easily spotting Laur, I watch her try to keep up with learning the line dance. A grin tugs against my lips, quickly followed by laughter. Laur struggles to keep up, frustration all over her face.

Keith pats my shoulder. "She's pretty terrible."

"Don't tell her that," I chuckle.

"I wouldn't dare," Keith replies, putting his hand to his heart in a theatrical manner.

Now is the perfect time to ask Keith what he thinks about Blaine. I need to make sure that I'm not the only one seeing it.

"This has to stay between us." I lower my voice, my smile forming into a serious line. "But can I ask you something?"

Keith's brows pinch. "Of course, man."

"Mitchell," I start slowly. "He seems like he's had a positive attitude change. Do you see it too?"

He nods. "He doesn't suck to be around anymore."

"Yeah, he seems to be turning over a new leaf." I pause. "But do you think it'll stick?"

I take a swig of my beer, nervous for his response.

Keith runs his hands over his face. "I don't know, man. Only time will tell."

Silence falls between us, the only sound is country music.

"Should we join them?" Keith suggests, pointing to the dance floor.

"Yeah, I'm game. I'm done with my beer." I toss my empty bottle in a trash can, following Keith to our group on the dance floor.

Unfortunately for Keith, the lesson portion is near over. If Laur has two left feet, Keith might somehow be worse. He's smooth on the ice, but the guy can't keep a beat to save his life.

Libby nudges Laur, gawking and pointing at me dancing. Even though it's been years, I already know this line dance well.

After the song plays twice through, the instructor announces that lessons are over. A slow song comes on, and regulars move to find partners to two-step.

Before Laur can walk off the floor, I take her hand to dance with me. Spinning Laur perfectly in a circle, I pull her close and begin to two-step.

Laur's eyes widen. "Where did you learn to do this?" She keeps up easily as I guide her along the dance floor.

"My mom forced me to take some random dance lessons when I was younger." The lie rolls off my tongue before I can process what I just said. Why did not tell her that my ex-girlfriend made me take lessons with her?

"This is the first time I've line danced," Laur says sheepishly.

I try to hold in my chuckle, but it easily escapes. "I didn't notice."

Laur rolls her eyes at me. "But you, you dance so well," Laur declares, wonder in her eyes. "Hockey player turned cowboy. Could you get any sexier?"

"Probably." I waggle my eyebrows at her suggestively. "I could take my clothes off."

"My eyes only." The same eyes narrow with possessive eagerness.

"That can be arranged," I taunt playfully, my voice low. "There are only single person bathrooms here."

Laur teases, playfully hitting my chest, "Maybe someday, cowboy."

"Someday?" Lust creeps through my body as my voice grows deeper with desire, dreaming about the possibility. "Why not tonight?"

"Lucas Donato." Her mouth hangs agape. "Who even are you? We are rule followers!"

"Maybe it's time we let loose." I grab her hand and pull her body to mine. I'm already growing hard against her thinking about having her right here in this bar.

Laur lets out a deep sigh. "Okay," she whispers.

"Seriously?" I ask, more surprise in my voice than intended. "I mean, are you sure?

She nods her head. "As long as we can be discreet. No one can know."

"Deal." I nod in agreement, desire dancing in my eyes as they meet hers.

"Five minutes," Laur says. "Meet me in the farthest bathroom in five minutes."

She turns to go before whispering and holding up three fingers. "Knock three times."

Knock. Knock. Knock.

I hear the sound of feet nervously shuffling on the other side of the door.

"Laur," I lean as close to the door as possible in hopes she can hear me. "I knocked three times like you told me to. Open up."

The door opens just a sliver before Laur's hand darts out. She grabs my shirt and frantically pulls me into the bathroom.

"Did anyone see you?" she whispers.

"The coast was all clear." I close the distance between us and pull her body to mine.

She releases a weary breath, putting her head on my chest. She's obviously nervous so I start slow and steady. Lifting her chin, I plant a soft kiss on her delicate lips. The second my lips leave hers, she yanks me back to her, kissing me like she's never kissed me before.

Her kiss is electric with this newfound hunger that instantly has my cock pulsing. Her tongue slips past my lips, eagerly searching for mine.

Breaking our kiss, I trail kisses along her jaw and neck, nipping and biting as I go.

"I want you," she whimpers, pulling at the button on my jeans. In one swift fluid motion, I shift Laur so her back is to my front.

"Good," I breathe into her ear, softly sucking it. Her breath grows rapid as I slowly trace my fingertips along the v-neck of her shirt, grazing her breasts.

My other hand finds the top of her jeans, skimming along the fabric's edge teasingly.

"Please," she lets out a quiet whine.

"Please what," I murmur. "Tell me what you want."

Without uttering a word, she unbuttons her jeans.

"Use your words, Lauren. Tell me."

"Put your hand in my god damn pants," she begs, "then bend me over and fuck me."

"Yes, ma'am." My hands are at the front of her jeans, helping her to ease them down her legs.

The second I touch her pussy, a moan ravishes from her throat, sending me over the edge. I claim her mouth with fire, my tongue tangling with hers in a reckless dance.

I slip two fingers inside of her, already wet with need for me. My fingers move slowly in and out of her pussy while my other hand cups her breast.

"More," she groans into my mouth. Her teeth sink into my lower lip making me lose it.

My finger come away wet with her need. Unbuttoning my pants, I lower them past my hips, one hand wrapped around my cock.

"Put your hands on the sink and bend over." I stroke myself, not taking my eyes off of her as she arches over for me. The sight of my girlfriend leaned over the bathroom sink, legs spread and waiting for me unleashes the heat I've been holding back. My self-control out the fucking window.

I line my cock up with her entrance, placing one hand on her ass. The head of my dick barely touches her but I can feel how ready she is for me.

"Holy shit," my voice is a low growl. "You are so damn wet."

"I know. Now see how dripping wet you can make me," she gasps as I thrust into her in one quick movement,

Her words ignite something deep inside me. Or maybe it's the feel of her slick walls around my cock. I drive my hips to meet hers over and over.

"Lucas." My name sounds like a wicked sin coming out of her mouth.

Her hips start to move in rhythm with mine. A guttural groan rises from my chest as I press deeper into her pussy.

"I'm so close," she cries out softly. My hand flies to her mouth to make sure she stays quiet. We are in public after all.

Her heat grips me, pulsing around me as she finds her release. She trembles with pleasure, making me instantly find my euphoria buried inside her.

"That was the exact thrill and stress relief I needed," Laur pants, kissing my cheek and motioning for me to hurry out of the single stall restroom.

A sly smirk slides across my face as I button my jeans. "Happy to be of service," I tease and quickly sneak out.

Chapter Nineteen
Blaine

My eyes scan the dance floor. There are some beautiful girls in insanely tight shorts at Howdy's, but my eyes keep drifting back to Libby. It has nothing to do with her radiant smile or the short skirt she has on. I really need to talk to her about what happened at the beach.

"This was a great idea," Syd giggles. She and Libby re-join us at the table.

"I agree," Lucas smirks. He disappeared for a while, and I assumed he went home.

"Where's Laur?" Libby picks up her drink that's probably now lukewarm.

"Bathroom." Lucas' eyes dart around the bar. "But I think we're going to head out soon."

"No!" Libby shrieks with a pout, "Syd and I want to dance more."

"I can take you home later," I suggest, "Most of the guys have already left, and I just had one beer tonight."

"Thanks!" Sydney grabs Libby's hand and drags her back on the dance floor before she can decline my polite offer. This is the perfect opportunity to get her to talk to me. I just need to find a way to distract Sydney and get Libby alone.

Laur and Lucas leave almost the second she comes back from the bathroom, leaving just me and Silas left at the table.

"Think we are going to do well this year?" Silas asks, trying to make casual conversation. Silas is a junior like me. We've always been friends, I guess. He never got in the way of my antics, and we've hung out here and there.

"I think we've got a really good shot at going all the way this year." I smile from ear to ear.

"Me too, brother." He takes a sip of his dark mixed drink. "Listen, I met this girl earlier. Is it cool if I leave to go hangout with her?"

"Yeah, man, do your thing," I chuckle.

He says goodbye and goes off to find the mystery girl he met earlier. It's just me, myself, and this room temperature beer I've barely touched left at the high-top table.

A new country song about liking brunettes comes on. It's so catchy that I can't stop tapping my foot.

"You like Trae West?" Libby asks, walking up with Sydney snagging their drinks off the table.

"It's a good ass song." I take a pull of my disgustingly warm beer.

"It's one of my favorites!" Sydney twirls around, her melted down drink now in hand.

"Mind if we stay a little while longer?" Libby's eyes plead as they meet mine.

"On one condition," I counter, "you slow dance one song with me."

"Don't leave me by myself," Sydney huffs.

A blond man taps her shoulder and says he will gladly dance with her. She makes a sound I'm not quite sure is human but it's definitely some type of excitement before taking his hand and going to the dance floor.

Libby slams her now empty drink down. "Fine, you have a deal, Blaine Mitchell."

We make our way onto the dance floor. She wraps her arms around my neck and we start moving to the music.

"So about what happened at the beach," I start but Libby cuts me off.

"Please don't tell me you're into me now." She rolls her eyes, which is no surprise.

"Hell no." The words fly out of my mouth. "You're like the sister I never wanted."

"And that you pretended to sleep with?" Her lip curls in disgust.

"Shut up," I chuckle. "I want to know why you had me cover for you."

Her shoulders rise and fall in a subtle shrug. "I didn't want anyone to know the truth, and you must have sensed it. I didn't really ask you to do it."

She's right. She didn't flat out ask me with her words but her pleading eyes begged me to save her with a lie.

"I didn't mind covering for you. I was just wondering."

Silence falls between us, and pretty soon, the song ends.

"I want you to be my fake girlfriend," I blurt out.

Libby blinks rapidly and her eyes widen.

"Let me explain," I say. "One more dance."

To my surprise, her arms stay wrapped around me. She's willing to listen.

"You know I have a . . . certain reputation," my pulse quickens with each word, "but I want to change that and I think having a fake girlfriend will help."

"How?" Libby narrows her eyes.

"I think it'll show that I can be serious. That I'm maturing." I'm making this up as I go along. I do think it'll help, but the *how* hasn't been thoroughly thought out. "Not being a fuck boy who gets into fights and who doesn't put his team first. Maybe make alternate captain."

"You really think having a fake relationship is going to do that for you?" she huffs.

My heart grows heavy knowing that it feels like an impossible feat, and I know there is a slim shot I would make alternate captain. But a slim shot is better than a fully blocked net.

"I've got to try." I look down at my feet, wanting to avoid her eyes.

"Look, I know I owe you for being a good friend," Libby says. "Can I think about it?"

Her response is better than I could hope for.

"Absolutely." A grin spreads from ear to ear. "One more question though. Am I supposed to act like we are together?"

"Why? What do you mean?" Her eyes lock with mine.

A heavy sigh leaves me. "It seems like since the beach everyone expects that we are kind of together. I'm not sure how to act honestly."

I feel lighter finally getting the words off my chest. I've been tiptoeing around unsure of how to respond to people or how to act around Libby.

"Can I think about that too?" There's a gleam of something I can't quite put my finger on in Libby's eyes.

I nod my head. "Whatever works, I'll just keep doing what I've been doing."

The slow song ends again. Over the speaker, it's announced that line dancing is going to start again. I have no interest in line dancing tonight, so I start to walk off the dance floor but Libby grabs my hand.

"Thank you again, Blaine. For covering for me," her voice is filled with gratitude. "I really do appreciate it."

Sydney comes running up behind Libby, grabbing her shoulders and bouncing with glee as the new fast past song starts.

"Can we please dance to two more songs before we leave?" Sydney pleads with eyes as big as the moon.

"Sure, I'll wait over there." I point to our table.

The conversation with Libby went better than I thought it would, but it left me asking myself if I've really put enough thought into what having a fake girlfriend would be like. Would it really help me redeem myself? I guess there's one way to find out.

Chapter Twenty

Laur

Jittery with nerves, I sit down in between Libby and the other senior on the team, Kat, in the conference room to orient them before the final round of interviews start.

"Remember we have five spots open," I remind them. "We want to ensure there are more underclassmen to grow into the roles but would be open to some junior candidates."

"We have me and two others," Libby mutters under her breath. "We don't need any more juniors."

Narrowing my eyes at her, I continue, "Ideally, we want a mix of those who have a background in sports or an affiliation with hockey, as well as candidates with an extensive background in planning events." I pause, nervously biting my nail. "If the events are more charity focused, that makes the candidate even more favorable."

I hand them each a packet of paper. "I know we've watched the recordings of the interviews, and that you've seen these details over email, but here are the nine final candidates we are interviewing over the next two days. Each get a maximum of one hour."

I force myself to keep in the long sigh itching to escape me, I ask the girls if they have any questions.

"Did you pick the order of the candidates for a specific reason?" Libby asks curiously.

"Yes, the first three are the strongest in my opinion," I explain. "The others I am on the fence about."

"Knew it," Libby whispers with a slight smirk.

"I thought Raven was a strong candidate?" Kat inquires, her brows furrowed.

"She has a strong background, but I'm not sold on her wanting to work in sports or hockey." I fold my hands together. "The two times I've asked her, she hasn't concretely answered why she is interested in pivoting toward hockey."

Kat taps her finger to her lips. "Interesting."

"If by interesting you mean weird," Libby mumbles, browsing through the packet I just gave her.

"I'd like to re-watch the recordings of the second interviews," Kat says. "Can we do that tonight?"

"Absolutely," I grin, loving her dedication.

Libby lets out a small groan. The next two days are about to be extremely long.

Less than five hours later, we've interviewed five of the nine candidates. The first two were less than thirty minutes, and we all agreed: automatic "yeses."

"We have three spots left if Lena and Emery accept," I remind them, the nerves in my stomach finally settling after the video calls. "I will send out emails to them tonight. Hopefully we will have an answer from them before we start the interviews tomorrow to know how many final spots we need to fill."

"Let's talk about the other candidates today. Is there anyone else we want to give an offer to today?" Kat asks.

Shaking my head, I take out my phone to order pizza. We are going to need fuel while we debrief and re-watch any old interviews.

Kat turns to Libby. "What did you think of Marci? I really think she would be a perfect fit."

"I'm surprised how much I like Marci," Libby remarks in a higher pitch than typical.

"What's not to like? She understands hockey and has a background in organizing volunteers," Kat gushes. "We would be stupid not to accept her."

Libby groans softly. "But do we really need another junior?"

Kat snorts. "Who cares what year she is? We would probably be better stacked if we had more than just Laur and me as seniors."

"Twenty minutes for the food," I chime in, ending my call. "Kat's right—class doesn't matter, experience does." I understand Libby's hesitation. She doesn't want competition to lead the program next year. Trying to reassure her, I add, "Besides, she said she would stay an extra year most likely anyways."

"Right . . ." Libby utters in a low voice.

"She's an easy yes for me," Kat announces before taking a drink of her water.

Turning to Libby, I ask, "If she wasn't a junior, what would your answer be?"

Libby hesitates, twirling her hair around her finger.

"C'mon, Libby," Kat complains. "Just give your honest answer."

"Fine. She's a yes," Libby blurts out.

Kat rolls her eyes at Libby's dramatic response.

"Great, then I will extend her an offer tonight also." Clasping my hands in excitement, I verify, "We are waiting to decide on the other spots until tomorrow, everyone agreed?"

Both girls confirm their agreement.

"Perfect." The exhausted sigh I've been holding in since we started finally weasels its way out of me.

"I agree with that too," Libby giggles. "Let's get to watching these other interviews so we aren't here all night. I'm assuming we want to watch everyone who's left?"

Kat gives an approving nod as I re-open my laptop and find the interviews on my computer. From the second I hit play, we all intently watch, taking notes on each of the girls we have not extended offers to yet. My stomach rumbles, thank goodness we ordered pizza.

"Two hours fly by when you're having fun," Libby jokes, stifling her exaggerated yawn with her arm.

"Raven is a top contender for me," Kat admits.

Libby inclines her head, "I might be with Kat on this one, Laur."

"The lack of answering the hockey question doesn't bother anyone else?" I inquire. My gut roils with unease.

"She kind of answered it," Kat explains. "She wants to pave her own path, it sounds like."

Libby takes a bite of pizza before saying, "Let's make sure to ask her hockey specific questions tomorrow. I'll re-ask the 'why hockey' question also."

My stomach still does small flips. Something just seems off about her answers, but if the other two agree she'd be a good fit, then I trust them. I give a slight nod before asking about the girl I favor.

"What are your thoughts on Lulu?"

"A little cross-eyed," Libby shrugs.

"Libby! Be nice!" I shout at her, wishing I had something to throw at her other than my pizza—I'm not willing to give up this last slice to prove a point.

"I'm sort of kidding," Libby mutters, "but I did think she had really put together answers in her last interview."

Kat chimes in, "I agree. Her answer for how to balance class with tight deadlines and pressure was flawless." She hesitates to say more.

"What?" I pry, wanting to know what more she has to say.

"Honestly—" Kat takes off her glasses and rubs her eyes. "—I'm just exhausted. Can we plan to regroup before we start interviewing tomorrow?"

"Good idea," Libby speaks up. "If I don't get to bed in the next two hours, I won't be able to function tomorrow."

With little conversation, we pack up our things and head home. Libby and I hardly say a word on our walk home or once we get into the house, besides a brief mutter of see you tomorrow.

Before taking a shower to rinse off the stress of the day, I send out three acceptance letters and emails. My stomach is still in knots. I'm ready to finally start with our new team. Wishing that with each drop of water from the shower head, my anxiety would wash down the drain.

Ding.

The sound of my email chimes while I brush my teeth. Checking it, I find that Lena has officially accepted.

"YES!" The shout erupts from me, but I quickly cover my mouth. Libby and Jaylin don't seem to stir from my loud excitement. Dancing my way to bed I mutter to myself, "One down and four more to go."

Tossing and turning, I can't seem to fall asleep. My mind races with the possibilities. Once sleep finally comes, worry filled dreams come with it.

I wake up in a panic from an awful nightmare where every single person we interview declines their acceptance. We don't have any new members.

I leap out of bed toward my computer, checking my email to make sure I didn't dream up Lena accepting the offer. Sifting through my crowded inbox, I finally find her acceptance and relief washes over me.

My jaw drops at two new email replies. Both the other girls accepted too! A happy dance takes over my body, three out of five. *We are so close*! I twirl and groove to my bathroom where I fill my empty water glass from the bathroom sink.

My eyes meet my tired reflection, but the bags under my eyes won't keep my excitement away. "You got this, Laur," I whisper.

Laying back down, I quickly drift off to sleep.

"Laur, you are going to do great," a soft angelic voice whispers to me.

"Laur."

"Laur, you are already doing amazing." The voice is still faint, as if it's far away.

"Laur, I am so damn proud of you." The voice becomes clearer. It's Nick.

"Laur."

"Laur."

Sitting up in bed, I realize the sound of Libby calling to me morphed with my brother's voice in my dream.

"I'm up!" I shout back. Heart racing and adrenaline pumping, I jump out of bed realizing I'm late and quickly throw on clothes. "Give me five minutes!"

I make sure to thoroughly brush my teeth. Thank God, I took a shower last night. Beaming from ear to ear, I rush down the stairs. The knots in my stomach finally untangled from the words I heard from my brother in my dream.

Kat taps her foot as we approach the meeting room in the arena.

"It's my fault!" I explain, sprinting to meet her. "I slept awful last night."

Libby loudly bursts in from the end of the hall, unable to contain her enthusiasm, " On the plus side, all three girls accepted last night!"

"Wow!" Kat's sour pout turns into a gleeful grin. "That was fast!"

"Are we ready?" Delight dances in Libby's eyes.

I breathlessly agree, panting to catch my breath from running down the hallway.

The first interview goes quicker than anticipated.

"If you can't come up with an answer for how you would handle a player forgetting about an in-game interview, then you probably can't cover the in-game interview yourself," Libby frustratingly huffs as soon as the call ends.

"That's a little harsh." I cross my arms. "She doesn't have much experience *and* would be a freshman"

"But it's accurate," Kat agrees with Libby, "even girls from your last round that we cut had better answers."

"Okay, she's a 'no,'" I concur.

"Raven's next?" Libby practically bounces down in her seat, looking at the printed out schedule in front of her.

"Yeah, I'm really looking forward to talking with her!" Kat exclaims with just as much elation as Libby.

Struggling with my lack of sleep, my body craves caffeine of any kind. "Does anyone want anything from the vending machines? I need a Diet Coke before we start the next one."

I hustle down the hall to get my caffeine fix.

"Diet Coke before 9:00 a.m.?" Lucas' voice makes my heart beat quicken.

"I overslept," I confess, turning to face him after grabbing the three diet sodas I purchased.

He cocks an eyebrow at me. "Enough to need three?"

"They aren't all for me obviously." I playfully glare at him. "How's early practice going?"

"Hasn't started yet," Lucas replies, "but I'm sure most of the guys seem more tired than you."

Of course, he got here early to skate and practice before everyone else.

"You're so funny." I hit him on the chest.

A boyish grin takes over Lucas' face, causing butterflies to emerge in my stomach.

"I think I'm funny."

His comment earns him an eyeroll.

"How are your interviews going," he asks. "Almost done?"

I breathe out wearily.

He chuckles. "That good, huh?"

Shaking my head, I explain, "No, they are going great. We already offered three spots yesterday, and they all accepted last night."

"That's amazing!" Lucas beams with pride, causing the butterflies in my gut to take flight again. "But why the long sigh then?"

"It's just exhausting," I tell him, "and there are few girls I'm still on the fence about."

"Listen to your gut, babe," Lucas advises. "It's always worked for me."

Before I can get another word in, Lucas says, "I've got to go. You've got this, Laur."

He kisses me on the cheek and quickly walks to the locker room.

What does my gut say? Is Raven the right choice?

Chapter Twenty-One
Laur

A wave of nausea replaces the butterflies that previously filled my stomach as we wait for Raven to join the call. She's two minutes late.

"Hi." A voice mixed with eagerness and regret comes through the computer speakers. "I'm so sorry I'm late."

Cutting her off right away, I tell her, "It happens. Let's drive right in since we have limited time."

"Great!" The word tumbles out, bright with excitement but still laced with guilt.

After taking a moment to introduce Libby and Kat, we start with questions.

Kat starts off by asking about how she would handle a player not showing up for a planned interview during a game, leaving her alone on the jumbotron.

Clearing her throat, Raven begins, "Before the game, I would confirm I know the opponent's current record and how we have historically played against them. I would want to make sure regardless of if the player shows up I understand how we stack up to them now and in the past."

Libby eagerly nods, a sparkle of amazement in her eyes as if she has a girl crush.

"I would want to highlight the key successes in the game so far," Raven continues. "Let's say this interview is during the first intermission. I would highlight two to three strong plays from our team."

Interrupting her, I ask, "What if we are losing?"

"Great question." Raven doesn't reply for a beat. "I'd talk about opportunities we missed where we could build strength or something from the previous game that was successful the team would attempt to capitalize on."

I'm about to interrupt again, but she keeps explaining. "Before the game, I'd want to sit down with whoever I am interviewing to understand what they see as opportunities and weaknesses for this game and what they view as the best success this season." Her voice carries a vibrant confidence. "That way I can have some player quotes as well as an expert answer on how we can improve our game."

"Fabulous idea," Libby remarks.

Kat chimes in, "Agreed, I've done that before some games actually."

Raven continues to elaborate more, but my attention is elsewhere. Both girls seem to be in awe of Raven's well-thought-out response. Is she as impressive as they seem to think?

Kat follows up with another question, but I don't hear what she asks. Taking a sip of water to calm myself, I paint a smile on my face. I'm being ridiculous.

Libby calls me out, bringing me back into focus. "Right, Laur?"

"Absolutely," I answer, not knowing what I'm agreeing to. Glancing at the clock, I inform everyone we have time for one last question and nod to Libby, signaling to her to pose the question.

"Raven, with your background focused on fashion, why are you interested in a program focused on sports marketing?" Libby maintains a serene demeanor, with no hint this question was rehearsed.

Raven twirls her hair around her finger. "Truthfully, I have had a lot of opportunities within the fashion industry because of family connections." Her voice is low with uneasiness.

She pauses, taking a long breath. "I want to distance myself and prove I can form an established PR career on my own." Her voice cracks at the end. "My mother has a thriving career in the fashion world, and I'm very lucky to have had opportunities because of her."

She pauses, taking a long breath before whispering, "She doesn't think I will be successful without her."

The conference room and the call fill with an eerie silence. Before I jump in to fill it, Raven continues.

"I don't want you to feel bad for me. I want to make a name for myself." Raven's voice shakes. "Growing up, I was around hockey a lot. My closest guy friends and family friends played hockey. Compared with other sports, I've been around it the most."

Taking a sip of water, I try to wrap my head and heart around the fact that not everyone can have blood ties to hockey like Libby and I do. Libby's cousins play college hockey just like Nick did.

Raven inhales sharply. "But I specifically applied to this program because of the large charitable focus. Helping to plan and execute charity events has been the most rewarding part of the experience I have. The Wyverns' program focuses on charitable events more than any other program I found."

Building back the confidence in her voice, she explains, "I looked at programs across multiple sports, but hockey I have the most familiarity with as I mentioned. The Wyverns' program really stuck out to me. Your work with the Nick Bellinger Foundation last year and giving back to the larger hockey community really amazed me."

"Without the Wyverns' program, the Nick Bellinger Foundation wouldn't have been founded," I respond, voice soft and airy.

"I might not have the most experience with sports, but I promise you—" Raven's voice grows steadier and stronger with each word"—I am extremely dedicated to making the world a better place through charitable work. It's my biggest passion."

"I can hear your passion," I assure her. "Thank you for sharing your heartfelt answer with us."

She would be such an asset to our team. I should have seen it more clearly before. Raven needs to join our team. I feel it in my gut.

We take a short break after hanging up with Raven. It's unanimous—we want to extend her an offer.

The last two candidates go very quickly, nothing wowing me. Although Libby and Kat are fond of one, we all agree that one of yesterday's candidates would be the best fit. I offer to stay to clean up the conference room and create the offer letters.

"Thanks for letting us leave early" Libby shouts as she opens the door. "I have a hot date tonight to get ready for!"

Raising my eyebrows, I inquire, "With Blaine?"

"No," She rudely snorts, leaving before I can ask any other questions.

Not my drama, I tell myself. *I have other things to focus on.*

Tension melts away the second I hit send on the offer letter emails. Turning off the lights, I pull out my phone to give Bren a call.

"Hello," a chocked-up voice answers my call.

"Bren, is everything okay?" Concern furrows my brows.

"No," she sobs. "Liam and I are on a break."

My heart sinks to my stomach as I exit the arena. Before I can get in a word Bren says, "I don't want to talk about it though. How did the interviews go?"

"Bren, are you sure?" I pry. "I'm always here if— "

"Yes, tell me about the interviews," She sniffles. "Distract me."

Slowly, I say, "Just sent out the final two acceptance letters."

Bren's usual bubbliness starts to shine through. "Congrats! That's so exciting. Any juicy stories about candidates?"

Turning the corner onto my street, I tell Bren about the first round of interviews and how terrible two girls were, barely able to form coherent sentences without rambling.

"I would have been one of them if I interviewed," I confess to Bren.

Seemingly back to her buoyant self, Bren disagrees, "Yeah right, you would not be anything close to that," She snorts. "You would have been the best interviewee in Wyverns PR history."

As soon as I make it home, I lay down in my bed. Then, I tell her about the girl who had no answer to the question about a player leaving you high and dry during a game interview. I devalue my weird feeling about Raven.

"What's her last name?" Bren's voice is laced with panic.

"Mathews," I respond. The alarm in Bren's voice causes my heartbeat to quicken. "Why?"

Relief seems to fill Bren's voice. "I used to know a Raven. She sucked."

I'm about to ask who this mystery Raven she knows that I don't is when I hear voices downstairs.

"Oh my god," I whisper into the phone and creep towards my door.

"What?" Bren probes.

I let out a giant yawn.

"Lauren Chip Bellinger, you better tell me," Bren demands.

The voices grow louder and the stairs creak. I peek out my bedroom door into the hallway, spying a short blond boy that is definitely not Blaine Mitchell follows Libby's into her room behind her.

"You cannot tell a soul," I swear Bren to secrecy.

"Cross my heart, and all that jazz," Bren jokes. "Spill the beans."

"Libby just got home with someone, and it's not Blaine."

"Holy shit," Bren exclaims so loudly I have to pull the phone from my ear. "I'll be taking that secret to the grave."

"Yeah right, you are the biggest gossip," I tease with a laugh.

Bren lowers her voice, "No but really, I don't want to be on Blaine's bad side"

I let out a giggle. "Me either, especially since he doesn't have one lately."

My eyelids start to flutter. "Hey, can I call you later this week? I'm about to pass out."

"Absolutely. Goodnight," Bren says quietly.

"Love you, Brennie Bean," I mutter.

"I'll love you more if you get the dirty details in the morning from Libby," Bren whispers.

The next morning, Libby stumbles sluggishly down the stairs. Alone. She doesn't say anything about her date or the guy she brought home.

Bren is going to be so disappointed in the lack of dirty details I have to share. Frankly, I'm a little bitter myself. Why is Libby being so secretive?

Chapter Twenty-Two
Lucas

Arriving at practice early, I'm met with the sound of skates scraping the ice. Who would be here before practice? No one on the team comes to mind, except maybe Ryder King.

Spotting the filled locker cubby, my eyes widen seeing that the culprit is Blaine Mitchell. I frantically put my gear on and lace my skates, eager to spy on him before hitting the ice myself.

Blaine bolts through the cone drills set up, executing his stick handling with precision I haven't seen him have before. Racing toward the net, he winds up, taking a slapshot that goes wide and hits the post. Quickly recovering, Blaine gains control of the puck.

Clapping, I startle Blaine, causing him to lose his balance. "Don't fall on your ass after that snappy rebound," I call to him.

Regaining his balance, Blaine skates over to the bench where I've been watching.

"Didn't know you were watching me," he mutters, scratching the back of his neck.

"What are you doing here?" I fold my arms.

"Same thing you are, I guess." Blaine shrugs. "Getting in extra practice.

Chuckling, I inform him I usually come an hour early to practice a few times a week.

"I'll let you have the ice then," Blaine quietly says.

My brows furrow. "Don't be ridiculous, dude." I pat him on the shoulder reassuringly. "Let's go. I'll play D."

Truthfully, my defense game is not nearly as strong as my offense. I'm much better at scoring goals than protecting the net. But I don't mind helping Blaine out.

"You sure?" Blaine asks, still speaking softly.

"Yeah," I respond firmly. "Just let me warm up a little bit.

Blaine follows me into some skating drills, keeping up as much as he can but always a hair behind me. Weaving in and out of the already set up cones, my heart and mind find peace as I glide on the ice.

"Alright, you shoot against me," I instruct Blaine, take a stance near the net.

Blaine's eyes bulge out of his eyes but his lips stay sealed.

"C'mon," I chirp. "Show me something."

He knits his brows before skating to the other end of the ice. My eyes watch his shoulders rise and fall taking in a long grounding breath.

Blaine moves swiftly towards me, but once he's close to the center line, my instincts kick in and I'm ready to attack. He has to know I won't take it easy on him.

As his eyes scan me, he continues to maintain steady control of the puck. Within a blink of an eye, Blaine tries to rush into the attack zone but my stick immediately secures the puck, not allowing him a chance to get close enough to shoot.

"Again," I order Blaine, passing the puck down to the other side of the rink for him to retrieve.

Without complaint, he listens and tries again. This time, I give up a little space, letting him near enough to shoot, but I block the shot.

Without saying a word, I send the puck down the ice again. Letting out a small sigh, Blaine obliges and scurries to the puck. Letting him in shooting range again, I intercept the puck on his shot again.

A loud tormented groan comes from Blaine. His eyes narrow and fix on me in frustration.

"Want me to shoot on you?" I suggest.

"C'mon, Luc," Blaine complains. "You're a two-way player. I can't beat you on defense or offense."

With an awkward chuckle, I mutter *thanks*. I don't take compliments well from my team, especially when it's about how I can play offense and defense equally well. I can slam down a block, but I anticipate defensemen's moves, rather than make them.

"Alright fine, practice getting rebounds then?" I ask, trying to think of something to work with him on where he won't feel intimidated. Blaine's always been a great player and he's improved his game a lot since last season, but since we haven't gotten along in the past I want to show him that it's over.

He nods in agreement, moving to grab a cone to set in the middle of the goal for me to shoot against.

Blaine snags rebound after rebound perfectly, even tipping a few into the net with a swift wrist shot, despite the cone taking up space.

Sounds of our teammates fill the arena as practice gets close to starting.

"Good stuff." I hold out my hand to Blaine for a slap handshake. "Keep pushing."

"Still can't beat you," Blaine mutters under his breath.

"You've put in a lot of hard work, it's obvious," I assure him. "Don't be so hard on yourself. You've never practiced with just me before."

Blaine's eyes meet mine, his tone serious. "Surprised you let me."

At that comment, a laugh escapes me. "Yeah well, you're less of a pain in my ass nowadays, Mitch."

Blaine's nervousness reminds me of myself the first time I was on the ice alone with Nick Bellinger. I was so intimidated by Nick I thought I'd fall straight on my ass. My game was sloppy but he never judged me. He saw potential in me.

Despite how much I couldn't tolerate him last year, I see so much potential in Blaine. Maybe I can be an impactful mentor for Blaine beyond being his captain and teammate, just like Nick was for me.

Once practice starts, my eyes dart every direction, watching the team practice and fucking flowing with happiness. We just kicked off our full practice schedule and the Wyverns might be in the best shape we've been in in years, and we made it to the semifinals last year.

Ryder King is always in the right place at the right time—great off-puck instincts. His "Nothing can stop us" attitude has already uplifted every single player, making them work harder and play better.

When Ryder and Blaine are on the ice together, they are a force to be reckoned with. Like gears in a machine, they move in perfect harmony, anticipating each other's moves almost flawlessly.

For the first time this season, my heart aches a little, wishing Liam and Conner were both back on the Wyverns instead of graduating last year. My mind dreams up a place where the five of us are on the ice. We'd be unstoppable.

I'm not the only one on the team that notices the on-ice connection or how much effort Blaine has put into his game.

"You think people will vote for Mitch to be an alternate captain with the way he's playing," I overhear someone ask.

"Fuck yeah," Silas responds enthusiastically. "Bro is fucking fire."

A few of the team nod. I might provide my thoughts to the coaching staff who have the final say, but team voting always is taken into consideration. Seems like Blaine Mitchell shed his old gear and left his old ways in the past.

Tyler lets out a huff of frustration, eyes narrowing as he watches Blaine on the ice. His disdain for Blaine is obvious, but if it starts to impact the team, he's going to replace Blaine as the thorn in my ass.

Coach blows his whistle, signaling for the guys to bring it in.

"Eight a.m. sharp tomorrow in the workout room," Coach commands. "Don't be late."

He turns to me, glancing at me and then back at the team with raised brows, urging me to chime in.

"You heard the man, don't be late," I back up Coach. "We don't want any extra suicides."

"Before you leave the locker room today, submit two or three players as alternate captains." Trilled murmurs and excited whispers go around the rink. "Don't fucking forget. And make sure you can read your handwriting," I order.

"Can we just write their number?"

"Silas, if you can't write clear enough for someone to read your damn handwriting, then, sure, write the jersey number." I pinch the bridge of my noise and let out a sigh. "As long as it's easy to tell who it is—that's what matters.

The murmurs around the bench grow louder.

"When will they be announced?"

"Next week," I clarify, my voice echoing authoritatively above the loud mutters of anticipation. "Make sure you all do it before you leave. The box is right next to the door."

Signaling for everyone to head to the locker room, the noise grows louder. For being a group of men, they sure like to gossip.

"And Harlan," I shout. "Don't fucking fold your paper thirty times like a nitwit. Just fold it in half."

Harlan chuckles, muttering, "Hope you make the right decisions on your alternates, Captain." He salutes me and heads into the locker room.

No fucking pressure.

Chapter Twenty-Three
Blaine

"Hey, Mitch," Ryder utters quietly next to me. "Think you'll make alternate captain?"

My shoulders rise in a silent answer.

"Before I met you," Ryder's voice grows louder, "I heard rumors."

Ryder gulps down half a water bottle before continuing. "Rumors that you were rowdy, ruthless," he pauses, taking another sip, "had a bad reputation."

My eyes narrow and meet his. "What are you getting at, Ryder?"

"Nothing, dude, just haven't seen any of that." Ryder slaps me on the bare back playfully. "I think you've got a good shot at making alternate captain is all."

"Really?" My voice nearly cracks as I struggle to conceal the tremor in my words, my heart pounding wildly.

"Yeah, Mitch," Ryder confirms loudly. "Give yourself more credit. You're a real playmaker out there."

With a hint of a smile, I ask, "Who do you think the other will be? You or Keith?"

Ryder chuckles, putting a hand to his heart jokingly. "You flatter me, Mitch."

Guess that's a no.

"Let's hit the town tonight," Ryder pauses, pulling his shirt over his head, "blow off some steam, meet some girls. Unless . . ."

"Unless what?"

"Unless you're still with that girl from the beach." Ryder waggles his eyebrows suggestively.

Am I still faking being with Libby? Lord knows I want to be fake dating her to keep myself from making stupid decisions and tarnishing my new reputation I'm trying to build. But every time I've seen her lately, she's ignored me.

"I've got plans with her tonight actually." I lie through my teeth. "But Silas will go out with you, won't you, Silas?"

Turning away from Silas and Ryder chatting about their new plans for tonight, I glance down at my phone and text Libby.

Me: Busy tonight?

"By the way," Silas whispers to me. "I voted for you." A loud smack echoes in the locker room from the ass slap Silas just delivered in congratulations to me. That better not leave a fucking mark.

After taking a long shower, I check my phone. No reply. I texted her ten minutes ago. Guess she doesn't think we are fake dating or even friends. My fingers fly furiously across my phone.

Me: We need to talk about this fake dating thing.

Me: You're either in or out.

Me: It's confusing, I don't know how to act when people ask me. And you started this shit lying to everyone.

Libby: Okay. We'll talk soon.

Libby: But not tonight.

At least my maybe fake girlfriend finally fucking responded.

Chapter Twenty-Four

Lucas

"**D**onato, hit the shower then meet me in my office," Coach Andres barks at me as soon as I enter the almost empty locker room.

Responding with a nod, my heart starts pounding and my chest feels tight. I scurry to the locker room hoping a cold shower will help ease my oncoming panic from Coach wanting to see me. I don't have a planned meeting with him. This morning, I planned to meditate before practice to ease my anxiety that's continued to heighten the closer we get to starting the season.

Droplets of cold water melt away my tension and my heart rate slows. No more slacking on my meditation, I need to get my stress under control. Risking having a panic attack in front of my team is not an option.

I force a calm over my body and will my legs to carry me to Coach's office, keeping my steps tight and controlled.

"You okay, Donato?" Coach inquires, cocking his head at me. "You're clenching your fist pretty tightly."

Dropping my fist, I take a seat in front of his desk. "Yeah, just a little tense," I mutter before sighing heavily.

"Take care of yourself, kid," Coach insists. "We've got a long season ahead of us, but it's a bright one."

Coach shuffles some papers around his desk.

"Ah, found it," Coach mumbles. "Not everyone has voted, but there are two clear winners from the team." Coach runs his hand across his mouth. "Maybe two or three runner ups that could be swayed by the remaining votes."

My eyes meet his, clear that he is waiting for me to respond, but I don't say a word.

He coughs, breaking the silence. "Donato, I can't read your damn mind. Are you going to tell me your recommendations or what?"

My voice barely audible, I mutter *sorry*. Clearing my throat and finding my voice I start, "Keith is the most obvious."

Coach gestures affirmatively. "He's got the most votes and is the first choice of everyone on the coaching staff."

The tension in my shoulders eases, knowing I made at least one right decision.

"The other two," I start slowly, building back my confidence. "I'm unsure of."

"Donato." Coach runs his hands slowly down his face. "Either you have the recommendations, or you don't. You've always been so sure of yourself. What's going on?"

Not wanting to elaborate on my steadily increasing pressure, I blurt out what my gut has been telling me, "Blaine Mitchell."

"My thoughts exactly." Coach looks at me appreciatively, smiling. "Blaine's really stepped up his game."

"Tyler Barret is the other person I was thinking," I offer.

Coach offers a subtle nod of approval. I clasp my hands together, feeling a deep sense of relief wash over me knowing that Coach Andres and I are on the same wavelength about Blaine.

"What about Ryder King?" Coach asks.

My brows raise in shock; I've considered Ryder. He's bound to be the best player on our team, but he just joined.

"With all due respect, you asked my opinion. My final two recommendations are—" taking a deep breath I finally make the decision "—Keith Hall and Blaine Mitchell."

"That's surprisingly what the votes are telling us so far too," he mutters under his breath.

"Alright." Coach Andres stands up, offering me his hand to shake. "It's settled. Keith Hall and Blaine Mitchell are the alternate captains this season."

As I awkwardly shake Coach's hand, the dark clouds in my chest that were starting to part are at a standstill the second I get back to my locker.

"Mitchell, are you sure you don't want to join us," Silas asks Blaine.

"C'mon, Mitch," Ryder practically begs. "You're my best wingman."

A huff of irritation escapes Tyler and storms away without saying a word. No one seems to notice except me.

With a shake of his head, Blaine denies them.

"Blaine fucking Mitchell, don't make me get on my knees and beg you," Ryder tries to convince him.

Blaine lets out a chuckle, tossing his towel into the basket at the end of the bench.

"I can see it in his eyes, dude," Silas plays along. "He's not fucking around."

Ryder starts to bend a knee to kneel before Blaine finally caves.

"Fuck," Blaine concedes. "I'll go." He places his hat backward on his head, his signature style.

"Thank, God." Ryder clasps his hands together in prayer. "I'm trying to get someone on their knees for me, not the other way around. No offense, Mitch."

Silas cackles, feeding into Ryder's ego as a sly grin spreads across Ryder's face.

From around the corner, Tyler yells, "What do you think you're fucking doing?"

Ryder looks around puzzled, brows furrowed. "Uh, making plans?"

"I was talking to Mitchell," Tyler spits each word out like they're toxic, stepping directly in front of Blaine, fist clenched.

"Huh?" Blaine responds slowly, "I don't know what you mean, man."

Tyler snatches Blaine's hat from his head and flings it down to the ground before aggressively stabbing him in the chest with his finger.

"Don't fucking hurt Libby," Tyler warns as he pokes Blaine sharply in the chest again.

Blaine balls his hands into fists at his sides. Instead of launching forward at Tyler, Blaine throws his hands up in defense.

"I'm not doing anything to hurt her," Blaine speaks up.

In the blink of an eye, Tyler lunges forward, pushing Blaine, who manages to stay upright on his feet.

"I heard you," Tyler snarls, his face reddening with fury. "Don't lie."

Blaine's knuckles turn white. His arms are stiff, as if he's holding back the angry storm brewing. I'm positive a fight is going to break out if I don't intervene. But before I can, Blaine tosses his hands in the air again.

"Just because I agreed to go out, doesn't mean anything," Blaine counters.

Ryder rushes to back up Blaine. "Yeah, dude, I practically had to beg him. He said no at first anyway."

Blaine moves to pick up his hat off the ground where Tyler threw it, but as soon as it touches Blaine's hair, Tyler whips it off his head again, this time chucking it across the locker room.

"You hurt Libby," Tyler hisses through clenched teeth, "I fucking hurt you."

Tyler charges, ready to attack Blaine again, but Blaine swiftly moves out of the way.

"Woah!" Ryder shouts, his voice echoing off the locker room walls

"Barret, my office." Coach Andres' voice booms with demand before Tyler can make another move. "Now!"

Tyler snarls at Blaine, clenching his teeth.

Without hesitation, my captain instincts quickly take over, placing myself between Tyler and Blaine. My eyes narrow, giving Tyler an icy death stare while he makes his way into Coach's office to get reprimanded. His dark brown eyes blaze with fury, no remorse in sight.

Tyler trudges off, cussing under his breath, each stomp louder than the last.

At least I know recommending Blaine over Tyler was the right move.

One solid decision down this season. A million fucking more to go.

Chapter Twenty-Five

Laur

The stairs creak loudly with tiptoed footsteps that sound nothing like either of my roommates. Why would they be tiptoeing at nine in the morning on a Thursday anyways?

Leaning as far over as I can to sneak a peak of the front door, I spy the back of a bulky redhead as he attempts to quietly leave.

My eyes snap open in disbelief. This is the second guy Libby has brought home. Has she always been this promiscuous? I wouldn't judge her, but now I am even more confused with her situation with Blaine.

Taking a sip of coffee, I turn back to my computer. Eager to finalize the welcome packets for the new PR girls.

Libby's shuffling feet trudge down the stairs.

"Good morning," Libby yawns, floundering her way to the coffee pot. Dark circles lay beneath her eyes, and her disheveled hair sits on top of her head.

Raising my eyebrows at her, I ask, "Late night?"

Libby presses her coffee against her lips. "Oh, but such a fun one." A devious smile creeps along her face.

"Well, we do have a lot we need to get done today," I remind her, which earns me a groan in response.

"I'm barely awake yet," Libby complains.

"The girls will be here in two days, Libby," I start, unsure why I need to explain myself. "We have a lot of prepping to do, and I want at least one fundraiser event solidified for them to start on right off the bat."

Libby meets my eagerness to work with an eyeroll.

Before I can open my mouth to lecture her, something hits the front door with a loud *whack,* followed by three more.

"What the hell was that?" Libby shrieks, running to the front door.

Telling her not to open the door is on the tip of my tongue as I hear the front door open.

"What the hell!" Libby cries out.

Silently, I send a prayer up that it's nothing dangerous. My heart races as I quickly move to meet her at the door.

"Someone just egged our house!" Libby wails. "Who would do that!" She throws her hands up.

My heartbeat doesn't slow down. "I . . ." My words get lost in my throat, "I have no idea." I breathe out.

"We need to clean it up as soon as possible," Libby declares, closing the door and moving to the kitchen to get supplies. "If it dries it can ruin the paint."

It seems like roles have reversed as I stumble, following Libby into the kitchen. Dish soap, sponges, and a bucket are pulled out from under the sink.

"C'mon, Laur," Libby instructs. "We need to spray it down with the hose, then scrub with soapy water."

Without a word, I follow her outside and wait for her to get the hose. After she's sprayed down our front door and porch, we scrub at the leftover eggs.

"How do you know how to do this?" I ask. Libby went from hungover into action mode in a matter of seconds. She knew exactly what to do.

Libby's eyes fill with tears, but she ignores me and keeps scrubbing. "At least we got to it right away. It won't cause any damage."

"Libby . . ." I slowly start. She clearly doesn't want to talk about it, but I'm not sure how to comfort her without knowing what's wrong.

Libby wipes a tear from her cheek. "This should be good enough. Let's go inside."

As soon as we get into the house, Libby rushes around the kitchen putting away our supplies and throwing away the sponges. Unsure what to do, I sit down at the table and wait until she's done.

Libby releases a big sigh as she pours herself fresh coffee and sits down at the table across from me.

"There were a few girls in high school that hated me." She peers into her coffee as if she sees the memory in the liquid. "They hated me because one of them had dated the boy I was dating."

"They egged my car once." Her voice is quiet, and tears roll down her face. "I didn't clean it fast enough, and it took off some of the paint."

"I couldn't get it touched up for over a month." With shaky hands, she lifts her coffee to her lips but instead of taking a sip, she talks into the cup, her voice slightly muffled. "Every time I drove it, I was humiliated. Everyone knew what happened."

She takes a sip of coffee, while wiping her tears with the other hand.

"But Drew—" she sniffs, "—the boy I was dating, picked me up from across town as soon as I broke down and told him how embarrassed I was." A small smile finds her face. "He was a good guy."

"Libby, I'm so sorry that happened to you." I place my hand on hers.

Wiping her nose on the back of her hand, she lets out a laugh. "But I don't think it's because of a guy now."

"What about Blaine?" My mind races with possibilities of who could have done this and why.

Libby shakes her head in disagreement, "No, it can't be because of him. We've barely talked, which is my own fault," she mutters the last part of her confession under her breath.

"What about the guy this morning?" I'm grasping at straws, but I don't know anyone that would do this to us.

Libby's mouth drops open. "You know about Brad?" She sips her coffee again, mumbling, "but I was so quiet last night."

"I heard him come downstairs this morning and saw him leave," I reply with a laugh.

"Can't be anything to do with him," Libby assures me. "I just met him last night, and he's only in town visiting family."

Libby gasps. "Could it be one of the PR girls that didn't get accepted?"

"No." I give her a quick shake of my head. "I haven't sent out the rejections yet,"

Libby's eyes widen. "Why not?"

"I just got the final acceptance last night," I defend myself. "I was waiting to make sure everything was squared away."

Silence falls between us as we both rack our brains trying to think of who would egg our house.

"Since the season hasn't started, it can't be any of Lucas' groupies," Libby teases.

"You know," I start, narrowing my eyes with annoyance, "could be one of Blaine's groupies if the season started too. What is going on with you two anyways?"

"I don't want to talk about Blaine." Libby dramatically jumps up from the table. "I'm going to take a shower."

I holler after her as she climbs the stairs, "Don't forget we are getting work done today!"

That was not the way I expected to start my morning—or the way I wanted my eggs either.

Chapter Twenty-Six
Laur

The smell of burnt coffee and cinnamon rolls fills the air in *Roast & Revelry*. After this morning's incident, my brain has been in a fog, and I needed a change of scenery and suggested Libby, Kat, and I meet up here. I'm still racking my brain on who the hell could want to egg our house.

"Didn't someone suggest something about banging up an old car with a hockey stick during interviews?" Kat inquires, sipping her latte.

"Too dangerous," I mutter. I'm only half listening as I frantically send the last of the rejection letters, wanting to ensure everything is communicated and nothing is left lingering.

"The picnic basket auction idea that one of the new girls had in her interview was pretty impressive," Libby remarks.

She's not wrong, but I want to hold on to that idea until the new girls come so it doesn't seem like we are just stealing their ideas.

"Let's wait on that one," I respond quietly, eyes still glued to my computer.

"The calendar obviously is happening this season," Libby declares.

"Do you have any thoughts?" Kat asks softly trying to get my attention.

Fingers snap in my face, causing me to snap my head up and finally look up from my computer at Libby.

"Sorry," I mutter. "Last email to send." My fingers type furiously, trying to rush.

Libby lets out an audible groan of complaint. Conversations come to a halt, and the only noises that can be heard from our table at the almost empty coffee shop are the coffee and espresso machines. How silly of me to think that she and Kat could independently come up with ideas without me.

"Okay." Pressing send on my last email, I look up again, dragging my eyes from Libby to Kat. "You were saying . . ."

Libby blinks rapidly, exaggerating each close and open of her eyes in what I can only assume is annoyance. "The calendar is tradition," Libby responds.

Tapping my finger on my lips, I ask, "But how can we make it even bigger and better this year?" After a beat of no response, I add, "That's the goal for anything we do: how can we elevate and expand on anything we've done in the past."

"Will you be the photographer again? It will definitely save us money," Kat suggests. "Unless we get someone to donate their time, which might be difficult."

She's right. It'll be hard to convince someone to donate their time. Bren and Suz tried in the past. But how can I lead the initiative and take photos at the same time? Libby might have been right when she mentioned her and Kat would be lost without me. They seem to rely on me too much. I'd be a nervous wreck if I trusted them to run the photoshoot smoothly.

My heart sinks into my stomach thinking about Bren. If she was here, it'd be a freaking breeze.

A big exhale escapes me. "We can reach out to photographers, and I can be a last resort." I take a sip of my now watered-down iced coffee. "It would be difficult for me to lead the photoshoot and take photos."

Libby furrows her brows. "We can help." Her tone, dry and curt.

"I think—" Kat pauses before slowly continuing "—I have an idea."

Grasping my hands in excitement, I'm eager to hear what she has to say.

"What if we auction off four or five spots to attend the photoshoot?" She starts.

"They can all be escorted around by someone from the PR team," Kat mutters in a quiet voice.

Kat has brilliant ideas but seems to always doubt herself. Being much more introverted than Libby and me, she never comes out and hasn't gotten close with our friend group. Sometimes I feel like I barely know her, but she is one of the most eloquent writers I've ever met.

"I love it! What else?" I exclaim loudly, earning me looks from two other customers in the coffee shop.

"We can do a raffle, so that people can enter as many times as they'd like," Kat elaborates. "Maybe cap it at ten entries if we need to."

A small grin blooms over my face. This idea could have legs.

"What if we also give them some type of prize?" Libby chimes in. "Like a picture with the full team."

"Or their favorite player," Kat suggests. "Who wouldn't want a picture next to a shirtless, oiled up Wyvern?"

My mind races at the negative possibilities. "We'd probably need them to sign something to make sure they don't fondle or touch the player inappropriately."

Libby gives me an "Are you kidding me" look, her eyebrows raised.

"You never know!" I defend myself.

Kat and Libby both nod.

The idea has barely formed in my head before I open my mouth. "What if we print a calendar special for each of the winners instead."

"Explain," Libby enthusiastically insists, leaning forward across the table.

A thrilling buzz fills the air around our table as we start to elaborate even more on the idea.

"Instead of a picture with their favorite player, I like the idea of with the whole team," I explain, my speech rapid with glee. "They would get the picture with the whole team and pick a specific month that they wanted it to be featured. We would print them a special version."

"That's genius!" Kat cheers.

"We would be able to charge more per ticket since it would cost more to custom print them," I expand on the idea further. "I like the idea of capping it at ten entries too."

Libby sets down her coffee with a *thud.* "And," she jumps in, "we can promote it at the games leading up to the shoot with signs, social media, and having the players mention it in interviews."

"Lucas would easily make a video for us to use on social media," I throw in, knowing I can probably get Tyler to as well.

Libby shrugs. "You know we can easily convince some of the other guys to also."

"What about Ryder," Kat asks. "He's going to be a hot commodity. Do you think we can convince him to make a 'promotional' video too?"

"One way to find out," Libby comments. "I'm sure his captain can be persuasive."

"Or your boyfriend," I tease, muttering under my breath.

"Not my boyfriend," she snaps. Libby's sharp eyes meet mine, but the fury quickly melts away. "But yeah, he is buddy-buddy with Ryder; I'm sure he could convince him."

My heart flutters. Not only will it showcase the team, giving them much more attention this season, but it'll also give me more to add to my resume when I start applying for jobs. This is exactly what I was talking about. Hopefully we can keep the bolder and splashier ideas coming. The calendar photoshoot this year is going to be hard to top for whoever runs the program next year.

Chapter Twenty-Seven

Lucas

Walking up to Laur's house, I notice small little things poking out from the grass. When I take a closer look, I realize they are broken plastic forks. Someone forked their house. How fucking weird.

The front door opens with a creak, Laur mentioned she'd leave it open for me when I asked if I could come say 'Hi' before I head to practice.

"Laur," I call walking into the empty kitchen. My eyes flicker with surprise when I hear the ice rattle in my coffee from my hand shaking. My nerves are in full force today with the announcement of alternate captains after practice. I thought seeing Laur would help calm me, but based on how jittery I am, I doubt anything will.

"Good morning!" Laur warmly greets me as she sprints down the stairs. The second she walks into the kitchen, she throws her arms around my neck and presses her lips to mine fervently.

"You might not be that happy to see me once I tell you what's outside your house," I mumble against her soft lips.

A crease forms between her brows in confusion. "What do you mean?"

A heavy sigh slips out. Hoping to soften the news, I hand her the iced coffee. "Laur, your house has been forked."

Confusion still lingers on her face. "What do you mean forked?"

Running my hand through my hair, I elaborate, "Someone put plastic forks in it and broke off the handles so they are hard to get out. It's just a stupid prank. It doesn't harm the lawn."

Her eyes widen, and she puts her head in her hands, "This is the second time this week someone's done something to our house."

Waiting on her to explain, I take her coffee off the counter and take a sip.

"We got egged," she mumbles into her hands, her voice hushed.

"Seriously?" My jaw tightens with frustration. Why didn't she tell me when it happened? And who the hell would egg her house.

As if reading my mind, she adds, "We don't know who it was and cleaned it up right away."

"If something else happens, you should call the police," I suggest.

Laur looks up at me, taking the coffee straight from my hand, "That's not something I feel like dealing with." She takes a long sip of coffee. "I have enough on my plate. The new girls will be here tomorrow."

"Just tell me if anything else happens at least?" I pull her into a hug, hoping to ease her tension despite my anxiety probably being twenty times worse than hers. Today might be the first day in a long time that I don't want to go to practice.

Her head nods against my chest.

"Thanks for the coffee," she mumbles into my chest.

"I've got to get to practice." I kiss her forehead before pulling away. "Some of the guys and I can help clean up the forks later tonight."

"Hey." She grabs my hand to stop me from leaving. "At the end of the day, Coach Andres made the decision, not you." She places her hands on either side of my face. "The team votes also backed up Blaine, don't be so stressed."

"You got this, Captain." She smiles at me, before planting a soft kiss on my lips and letting go of my face. "Try to enjoy practice."

Like always, she's right. On the plus side, I don't have to make the announcement myself; Coach will do it.

When I'm about a few blocks away from the arena, I veer off into a side street to find a bench or quiet place to try to meditate and clear my mind. Our house was rowdy this morning and I couldn't concentrate with the noise of the boys chirping at each other.

Finally finding a bench, I sit down, closing my eyes lightly, breathing in deeply and letting out a massive sigh full of my anxiety. Thumbing through my phone, I find my free mediation app and press play. Calming chimes and a peaceful voice take over the music in my headphones.

Closing my eyes again, I try to focus only on the guide's soothing voice and let the world melt away.

Someone rapidly taps on my shoulder. My eyes open to Tyler's narrowed gaze and knitted brow starting down at me. Fucking great. The last person I want to see right now. Is he going to avoid me at all costs once he finds out he isn't alternate captain?

"Dude, what are you doing?" Tyler asks.

Flustered, I mutter something about a voicemail, abruptly getting up.

"I'll deal with it later," I mumble and walk off towards the arena.

Tyler quickly catches up to me, but I keep my headphones in. We silently walk side by side to the arena. Guess I won't get in my meditation before practice, and I really needed it today more than I have in a while.

The locker room buzzes with conversation when we enter.

"Donato, could have used your pressure on the ice before practice," Mitchell calls to me. "Mind if we grab some time next week?"

Since my stomach has been doing flips since Coach solidified his decision and knowing he would announce captains today, I didn't come to practice early for once.

"Sure thing, Mitchell," I reply with a curt nod, ready for practice to be over before it even started.

Mitchell gives me a wide grin. "Appreciate it." He taps me on the back before exiting the locker room.

His dedication compared to last season is a complete one-eighty. But if it helps the team, I'm in no place to question it.

Thankfully, I only had some sips of Laur's iced coffee for breakfast; my stomach knots deepen during drills. I almost lose my grip on my stick more than once from my clammy hands. I really need to pull it together before someone notices.

Before we start scrimmaging, Coach demands every player go back into the locker room.

"I know you are all chomping at the bit to know who the alternate captains are," Coach Andres' deep voice booms. My heartbeat races like a car around the tracks at Daytona. He isn't supposed to make this announcement until the end of practice.

"The team and coaching staff all seemed to unanimously agree on the same two players." He continues, his eyes falling on me. "Congratulations, Keith Hall and Blaine Mitchell."

Cheers and praise fill the locker room. Finding Keith, I give him a firm handshake. Chuckling, Keith pulls me into a hug.

"You deserve it, brother." I congratulate him, giving him an excited pat on the back.

The celebrations are short lived as Coach yells at everyone to hurry back to the ice. I can't seem to find Mitchell to commend his success too. Looking around the almost empty locker room, my eyes fall on Tyler, his eyes outrageous slits.

"Look, Tyler," I start toward him, but he furiously storms out of the locker room, hitting my shoulder with his.

Rubbing my shoulder, disappointment replaces the anxiety in my gut. Every time he makes a stupid decision, he just reassures me I made the right one recommending Blaine over him.

Once I'm back in the arena, I see Blaine already on the ice skating with Ryder. He catches my eye, and a smile beaming with pride takes over his face as he nods in thanks at me.

Our scrimmage starts off smoothly. Coach hasn't switched up lines much, Ryder and Blaine always running the ice together. Blaine impressively wins almost every faceoff he takes, while Ryder swiftly finds his passes. But no goals are scored in the first portion.

"Donato," Coach Andres calls, "Switch lines with Hardy, I want to see you play with Ryder and Blaine."

Taking over the faceoff, I protect the puck and pass it back to Mitchell, who is ready and waiting. He skates up the ice, making a flawless pass to Ryder, who's wide open but quickly swarmed by the other team's defense. Panicking, Ryder snaps the puck back to me. My heart races when my eyes find the opportunity to shoot. Winding my stick back, my slap shot hits the puck but it's deflected by Keith.

Blaine is quick on the deflection, taking control of the puck, skating behind the net and tipping the puck across the line with a beautiful wrist shot.

A blur comes at Blaine out of nowhere, knocking him to the ground.

"Tyler, what the fuck?" Ryder shouts, moving quickly to get Tyler off of Blaine. My skates carry me toward them, ready to intervene but Keith beats me to it, helping Ryder restrain Tyler.

Trickles of blood fall to the ice from Blaine's now split lip.

"Barret, my office!" Coach barks. Each of his words is louder than the last. "Practice is over."

In a protective stance, I stand in front of Blaine until Tyler is off the ice, then offer Blaine a hand to help him up.

"I'm good," he mutters, touching his lip and inspecting the blood that comes away.

"He's just pissed he's not alternate captain," Ryder says, skating up to him.

"Ryder's right," I murmur.

"It's no big deal," Blaine grumbles. "I've punched plenty of people. Probably my karma."

He chuckles and skates off the ice with Ryder by his side.

Tyler has every right to be pissed, but taking it out on Blaine is a fucking stupid move. Even though he might be one of the strongest players, I can't help but hope Coach benches him for at least two games.

I feel bad for Blaine. He doesn't deserve Tyler's wrath. Last year, no one tried to beat the shit out of anyone when alternates were announced. An unexpected thought comes to me.

"Party at my house tomorrow night to celebrate the new alternate captains," I shout as soon as I walk through the locker room doors. I might not be a partier, but Keith and Blaine deserve a celebration.

Chapter Twenty-Eight
Laur

Springing out of bed, I barely notice the lack of sleep I got the night before until I spot my puffy under-eyes in the mirror. I'm unsure if I tossed and turned last night from thrill or nerves, but either way, the new girls will be here in just a couple of hours.

The past few weeks of application review and interviews have been truly exhausting. Today it will make everything worth it.

"Laur," Libby calls from down the stairs, "are you almost ready?"

The welcome packets are close to being done, but I wanted to add in a calendar of events last minute so the girls can plan ahead. I planned to finish it last night, but someone threw a fork or a few hundred in my plans. Lucas and Keith came over to help Libby and me, but it still took hours to remove the plastic forks from our lawn. What happened to good old fashioned TP-ing?

After zipping my jeans, I open my closet to find something to wear. Today is important, so I ditch my usual leggings and oversized T-shirt to look more professional. While I sift through my closet, I find the flowy black chiffon tank top I was looking for, but my eyes linger to what's behind it—one of Nick's old Wyverns jerseys.

Pulling it out of my closet, I hug the jersey tightly to my chest. Tears pool in my eyes, but I try to quickly blink them away not wanting to ruin my makeup.

"I hope I'm making you proud, big brother," I whisper into the jersey, tears making their way down my face.

"Laur!" Libby shrieks again. "If you don't hurry, I'm going to go get coffee without you!"

"I'm coming," I shout back, my voice shaky.

Quickly, I rush into my bathroom. My makeup brush tickles my face as I touch up my makeup and hide my tears. Good thing I use waterproof mascara.

Five pairs of eyes I've only seen over a computer screen stare back at me as I walk to the front of the conference room I booked in the arena. Taking a quick calming breath, I paint on a smile and turn around to greet them.

"Hi, everyone," I start in a higher pitched tone than normal. "You probably recognize me from the interviews but hi." I give an awkward wave of my hand. What am I doing? Why would I wave?

Clearing my throat, I continue, "I'm Lauren Bellinger, the lead on the PR and marketing team, but please, call me Laur."

We start with introductions for both the returning and new members, getting everyone comfortable. Libby hands out the welcome packets to all the new girls.

"Newbies, you can go through the welcome packet on your own time this week." I begin to explain the mounds of paper being handed out. "The other packet is a brief calendar and information on key events throughout the season. This is a work in progress. We'll add to it throughout the year."

Kat passes out the calendars and event detail packets, still fresh from the printer. It took us all morning to finalize them.

"We have two big fundraiser events this year, but we'll be looking to add a third," I go on, enthusiasm lighting up my tone.

Signaling to Libby to take over the conversation, she begins talking about the calendar and the new changes we add this year.

"This idea is brilliant!" A junior who's been on the team for a while confirms.

"If I wasn't on this team, I would enter," another girl mutters, causing giggles to break out amongst the girls.

Pride fills my soul at the feedback. My smile grows wider, taking up my entire face.

"The other event—" I take back over "—was actually an idea that one of our new members pitched during her interview."

Whispers go around the room mixed with the sound of pages turning quickly as girls scan the materials looking for the event, hoping it was theirs.

My voice comes alive with energy as I continue, "Raven, incredible job pitching the idea to do a charity picnic with a player auction."

"Wow," she whispers, her voice barely audible. "Thank you."

My eyes find the young blonde girl sitting in the back of the room. Her bright green eyes grow wide with the news. As they meet mine, a glimpse of something like fear flashes in them, but she quickly looks down at her packet. My pulse quickens as unease washes over me. What was that? Is she just shy?

"The timing for the calendar is set in stone but the player picnic is tentative," I proceed, shaking off the strange feeling before it can take root in my gut. "We are aiming for the picnic to be mid-season and plan the third big event near the end of the season."

Pausing, I take in the room filled with girls I will lead for the next ten months.

"Each one of you will play a role on this team and make an impact, just like players would on a sports team." My smile comes back to my face, finally reciting the lines I rehearsed in my head, "It's a team sport. We will have to work together to make the hockey team look great, drive sales, and raise money."

"It will be hard work." My words rush forward, bright with my excitement coming back. "But I promise it will be rewarding, and we will have more fun than you imagined."

"Speaking of fun—" Libby boldly interrupts "—tonight there's a party at the captain's house to celebrate the new alternate captains." Libby steals my thunder sharing the news of the party. "Oh and the captain is Laur's boyfriend," she adds bluntly.

The mood in the room changes, electric and eager with energy.

"What do we wear?" someone whispers. I assume it's a new girl.

"Can we drink?" someone else mutters.

"Do we have to go?"

The room instantly goes silent at the last question.

"Why would you not want to go?" Libby sneers, putting her hands on her hips. "You get to hang out with the team and—" I cut her off, worrying, creasing my brow at what she will say next.

"You can wear whatever you want," I start.

"But it's a party so —" Libby goes quiet as my eyes find hers, meeting her with a menacing glare. Message received, she doesn't finish her sentence.

"Yes, it is a party," I declare. A new-found authority takes over my voice, "but you can wear whatever you want. What other questions do you have?"

Reluctantly, a redhead I recognize from interviews as the freshman Lena raises her hand.

"Yes?" I nod toward her, encouraging her to ask the question.

"Can we . . ." Her voice is like a whisper in the wind. "Can we drink?"

Fidgeting with my hair, I'm not sure how I want to respond. How the hell did I not anticipate this? Underage girls are going to want to drink at parties, but I don't want to encourage illegal behavior.

What would Bren do? Who am I kidding . . . she would probably hand them a shot.

What would Nick do . . . if it was his hockey team and a new player asked.

"You can do whatever you want," I blurt out, speaking way too fast. I take a sip of my watered down iced coffee, trying to find words. "I mean please be responsible, but what you do is your choice." My head nods as if I'm agreeing with myself. "Just remember you can get kicked off this team should your behavior get out of hand."

Lena's eyes grow wide as saucers with fear. Shit, I didn't mean to scare her.

"What she means is—" Libby jumps in to rescue me "—don't get sloppy drunk and don't get arrested. Any other questions?"

No one speaks up, but I am positive someone asked if they have to go. Maybe they are too afraid to ask in front of everyone.

"If you do, feel free to ask me after or send me a text," I offer. "We'll meet again later this week—details are in your schedule packets."

"Someone will text you details about tonight!" Libby squeals, clapping her hands in excitement.

Animated chatter drifts all around as the room slowly clears, but one girl lingers behind.

Sensing she wants to talk to me, I tell Libby to go ahead and I will meet her at home.

"Lauren," Raven says in a low voice. "I mean Laur."

"What can I help you with?" I paint a friendly smile on my face, trying to make Raven feel like she can confide in me.

"Is the party mandatory?" Raven rushes to explain herself, "It's not that I don't want to go or that I don't like parties. It's just that my sister is a freshman and already on campus for orientation, so my family is here too."

"It's definitely not mandatory," I confirm. "Only the meetings and dates in the schedule are mandatory."

"Are you sure? I want to go, it's just that my family will be gone," her voice trails off.

"There will be plenty of parties if that's what you're worried about," I say, trying to reassure her. "Enjoy the time with your family."

"Okay." She nods slightly, as if convincing herself she is making the right decision to see her family. "Thank you."

"Anytime." I give her a pat on the arm. "We are thrilled to have you on the team."

Chapter Twenty-Nine
Laur

Lucas' backyard buzzes with music, chatter, and plenty of people when I walk through the gate. Two kegs sit on the patio with people I don't recognize surrounding them. Groups of people stand on almost every inch of the grass.

"Do you see any of the new girls?" I ask Libby, thankful we came together because I don't see any of our friends or anyone from the PR team either. Everyone seems to be a stranger.

"No," Libby confirms, standing on her tippy-toes trying to peer around the backyard. "But let's go to the kegs. I'm sure there's someone we know around there."

"You made sure to tell the newbies not to come alone right?" Anxiety takes root in my stomach thinking about the new girls walking into this party full of people they don't know.

Libby huffs dramatically. "They're adults. I'm sure they wouldn't come alone anyways." She starts walking towards the patio and drinks. "Especially since they don't know anyone but each other," she mutters under her breath.

The sass Libby gives off radiates heat. I swear she used to be more chill and down to earth.

"I see Blaine!" Libby yells, grabbing my hand and weaving through the crowd waiting by the keg.

"Blaine," Libby squeals like a schoolgirl, throwing her arms around Blaine's neck. "Congratulations! I'm so proud of you, boo."

Libby takes Blaine's face in her hands, and plants a quick, mischievous kiss on his lips. He noticeably winces.

Before Blaine says anything, she rushes off. "We aren't waiting in this shit," she calls back to me, "going to grab a beer inside for us."

Blaine's eyes fill with wonder and confusion, seemingly stupefied by Libby's kiss as he watches her abruptly run off. Now, I can see a harsh cut running across his bottom lip. *What the hell happened?*

"What the hell was that?" Blaine mumbles, his stunned gaze meeting mine.

"Your guess is better than mine," I respond, truly unsure what Libby's intentions are with Blaine.

"But you live with her," Blaine mutters into his solo cup before taking a drink. "You know her better than me."

With a sigh, I explain, "Trying to understand Libby's romantic life is like trying to understand . . ." I pause trying to find the words.

"A maze with no exit? The Matrix movies? Why people like football more than hockey?" Blaine ponders.

"All of the above," I giggle. "But I was going to say rocket science."

"Ah well, I'm going to be a rocket scientist if hockey doesn't work out," Blaine says with a cheeky grin. "So women are much more confusing to me than rocket science."

A gleam of intrigue lights my widening gaze. "Oh," I stammer, at a loss of words, "I didn't know."

"That's because I'm kidding," he chuckles. "Last I saw Lucas, he was over there." He points to the left.

My face turns red, embarrassed at how gullible I was, but I mumble my thanks. Wanting to ask about his lip, I finally remember this party is for him.

"Congrats, by the way," I stumble over my words, dumbfounded that it took me this long to say it. "You deserve it."

Blaine nods in thanks.

"I mean it." I bite my lip knowing I'm about to say too much. "Lucas knew at the beach it would be you and Keith. You earned it, Blaine."

Patting him on the shoulder, I whisper softly, "Just don't tell him I told you that."

"Thank you." Blaine raises his glass to me in a salute.

As soon as I muster the courage to ask Blaine about his split lip, Libby reappears out of nowhere.

"I found Tyler." She hands me a beer bottle. "C'mon."

"See you later then," Blaine mumbles under his breath, walking in the opposite direction Libby pulls me to.

Tyler and Keith stand under the biggest tree in the yard with some other players and plenty of girls, two of whom I recognize as new girls on my team, Emery and Lena.

Greeting them warmly, they thank us for inviting them and including them.

"This party is awesome," Emery says. Her eyes dazzle with amazement.

"The guys are all so nice," Lena chimes in.

Out of the corner of my eye, I spy a wicked grin forming across Tyler's face.

"Great, I'm glad you're enjoying yourselves," I respond with a smile.

"Lulu just got here." Lena nudges Emery. "Let's go find her." Both girls go off to find the other new freshmen. A gentle warmth blossoms in my chest seeing how they quickly became friends.

My eyes meet Tyler's. The smug smile still on his face turns my friendly gaze to a sharp glare.

"What?" Tyler throws his hands up, trying to feign innocence.

"I didn't say anything," I retort, sipping my beer.

"Your look said it all," Tyler claims and moves to stand next to me.

"Stay away from my new girls, Tyler." I jokingly threaten him with a poke.

"But they're hot and think I'm nice," Tyler groans.

"Do I have to stay away too?" A voice from behind me asks. Ryder meanders over, a cocky grin tugs at his lips.

"If I have to, you have to," Tyler declares, furrowing his brow at Ryder.

"Just don't cause any issues," I scowl at them, "or you're on my shit list."

"Why is it okay for Ryder to talk to them?" Tyler retorts his voice loud

"You can talk to them all you want," I shrug, "Just don't—"I pause thinking of the right phrase to use without being crass"—pursue them."

Tyler folds his arms, offended by my orders not to make any moves on my girls.

Laughing, I explain that Ryder is at least a freshman and so are they.

"Not fair," Tyler claims, arms still folded. "Wipe that arrogant smile off your face Ryder before I do it for you." Tyler's voice goes cold.

"Hey, man, I can't help how old I am." Ryder nonchalantly laughs. "Don't give me a fat lip like you did Blaine."

So that's where Blaine's split lip came from: Tyler. My blood pulses as anger fumes within me. Tyler has gotten into more fights this summer than I've ever seen him get into.

"There you are," a soothing voice sings sweetly. "I've been looking for you."

Lucas turns me toward him. I turn back to unleash my frustration at Tyler, but he darts off the second he sees the opportunity.

"Urgh," I let out in frustration.

Lucas' brows crease with confusion. "Not happy to see me?"

"Of course I am." I wrap my arms tightly around him in greeting. "I just wanted to yell at Tyler for being a douchebag."

Lucas' laugh tickles my ear. "Just in general or . . .?"

"Why didn't you tell me he got in a fight?" I demand in a sharp tone, breaking out embrace.

Lucas runs his hand through his luscious hair before answering, "This is the first time I'm talking to you since this morning, Laur."

He's right. I'm being absurd. "Sorry," I mutter. "I'm just heated."

"If it makes you feel any better, Coach benched him for the first three games of the season," Lucas informs me.

"Am I a bad person if that does make me feel better?" I look down at the ground, feeling uneasy that I would wish something bad on my friend, but he needs to learn a lesson before he goes too far.

"Not at all." Lucas pulls me into another hug, pressing a gentle kiss on my forehead. "It sucks for the team, but he deserves it."

"How's the party?" I change the subject. "Seems like a pretty big turnout."

Lucas sheepishly puts his hands in the front pockets of his jeans. "I don't know half of these people. But yeah, everyone seems to be having fun."

"You're not having fun?" I ask, raising my eyes at him.

"I'm having even more fun now that you're here." A slow smile spreads across his face, his eyes crinkling at the corners. "Tell me about your day."

A big exhale pours out of me. "It's been long." I take a sip of my almost empty beer. "But we have a great new event planned for this year."

My heart races with excitement, I haven't told Lucas anything about our new PR plans this year.

"Already?"

"Yeah." I beam up at him. "It'll be an auction, but instead of just the players, it'll be a player with his curated picnic basket." My words spill out of me, eager to share more. "It'll be a new way to do player auctions without feeling like we are just auctioning off boys. Raven—"

"Raven?" Lucas interrupts with an edge to his voice.

"A new girl on my team."

"What's her last name?" he asks. His mouth is a fine line, and his jaw grows tight.

Why is he asking so many questions about her?

Chapter Thirty

Lucas

My heart tumbles into a pit of dread when the name Raven casually rolls off Laur's tongue. Concern fills her voice

"Her last name—," each word out of Laur's mouth is slow, her tone cautious, "—is Matthews."

The hollow ache spreading through my gut stops, I can finally breathe again. My ex-girlfriend's last name is her fashion guru mother's maiden name: Harrington. I'm sure if it was Raven Harrington, gossip would be spreading like wildfire, and I would already know about it.

"I used to know a girl named Raven," I mutter, knowing I owe Laur an explanation. "She's not someone you'd want on your team."

"Oh," Laur's voice is still laced with concern, but I quickly change the subject back to the event.

"Sounds like a great way to avoid the scandal that Brad Mancheto caused with . . ." I pause. "I can't even remember whose stepmom it was. But we haven't had a player auction since then."

"Exactly." Laur beams with pride. "After the secret auction is over, the winners would be in a big open area with the player and their basket. Everything would be easy to monitor and all very public."

"Secret auction?" My voice is laced with curiosity.

"Each player would curate their own basket, but it would be anonymous," Laur explains, a thrill of excitement in her tone. "You don't know whose basket you are bidding on. That would add an extra layer of discretion to really ensure that there are no sandals"

"It seems great in theory." A chuckle tumbles from my lips thinking about the guys trying to make picnic baskets.

Laur's nostrils flare in frustration.

"The guys might not be great at putting together biddable baskets." I stumble over my words, scrambling to ease her disdain.

Laur's shoulders rise and sink with relief. "If that's the only concern, then we are golden. My team would, of course, help with that."

Of course they would, Laur has really thought of everything.

"Then it's a perfect plan." A proud smile tugs at the corners of my mouth. "Your ideas are always brilliant."

Her face turns scarlet. Twirling her hair around her finger, she says, "It was Raven's idea."

Gravity yanks my heart downward at the sound of that name again. How am I going to get used to hearing that? Can she go by Ray or something?

Taking a long sip of my drink, I try to calm my nerves. I'm being ridiculous. It's just a name.

"But you will bring the idea to life brilliantly," I brag. "You always do."

A wide, famous Bellinger smile takes over Laur's still scarlet face as she mutters *thank you.*

"How was practice besides . . ." Laur trails off, clearly trying to keep the conversation going but not wanting to bring up Tyler again.

"Besides Tyler wreaking havoc?" I finish her sentence. She nods sheepishly, twiddling her thumbs. At least she finally sees that Tyler isn't the picture-perfect, gentlemanly guy she thinks he is. Her rose-colored glasses are starting to come off.

"Great actually." I let out a loud sigh. "Coach Andres announced the alternate captains halfway through practice instead of at the end." I shake my head in dismay, still disappointed at Tyler's reaction, but if Coach had waited until the end of practice there wouldn't have been any issues.

"Anyways, Coach is trying out some new lines, and I think we will be even better this year than last year."

A spark of joy dances in Laur's eyes. "Really?"

"Really," I confirm. There's warmth in my voice that I can't hide, but I feel ten feet tall whenever the realistic possibility of the Wyverns being better than this last year crosses my mind.

"We have so many other ideas for this year too." Laur's excitement spills out of her, her voice higher than normal. "We raised so much money with Nick's special jersey last year that we are really going to have to go big this year."

My eyebrow arches, intrigued and wanting to know more about these other ideas.

"What kind of other ideas?" I ask, my voice low. "Anything more you can share with your boyfriend?"

"So you're asking as my boyfriend and not as the captain of the hockey team?" She confirms, her eyes narrow at me suspiciously.

"Yes, of course," I respond in a husky tone. "Just as your endearing boyfriend."

A playful grin slides across Laur's face. "It might take some convincing."

Keeping my voice low and sultry, I respond, taking a step closer to her, our bodies almost pressed together. "I can be convincing."

"Trust me." Laur runs her gaze down my body and back up to meet my eyes. "I know."

"So, what other ideas?" I pry.

"Well," Laur tells me, "the new girls had plenty of incredible ideas during their interviews."

The mention of the new girls breaks my coy energy.

"Want to grab another beer?" I ask, craving more liquid courage if we are going to keep talking about this new girl Raven.

Laur tilts her head in agreement.

"I'll go grab them for us." I kiss her passionately on the lips, not wanting her to suspect anything after our flirty banter, before I make my way to the crowded kegs.

My eyes trail Blaine as he goes inside the empty kitchen alone. Is he trying to leave his own party early?

After pouring two beers for Laur and me, I look up and see Libby head into the kitchen. Good. He deserves to have some fun and celebrate tonight after the day he's had.

Chapter Thirty-One
Blaine

Everyone expects me to be the good-time party-boy. They also all assumed I'd be out back flirting with some girl, or I guess now they expect me to be talking to Libby but I find myself leaving the backyard in exchange for the somber silence of the empty kitchen.

Since getting back from the beach, I haven't been able to think straight. On multiple occasions, I've tried to talk to Libby about what the hell I am supposed to be to her, but she dodges the questions and barely responds to my texts. Am I supposed to keep pretending that we're hooking up or am I supposed to pretend to let her go? Either way, I'm pretending, which is nothing new to me.

As if on cue, Libby strolls into the kitchen as if on a mission. "There you are. Did you find your next conquest yet?"

"What's that supposed to mean?" I sneer at her, folding my arms. "Conquests are your thing, Lib."

"Oh please, don't pretend like I'm some kind of heathen and you're a saint. I know you, Blaine." Her eyes narrow to a sinister glare. "My . . . extracurriculars . . . are no different than yours."

Know me? My fists clench in frustration at her assumptions, and it takes every ounce of self-control not to scream the question in her face.

She doesn't know me at all. No one on this campus does. I'm not heaven sent by any means. But Libby doesn't know that I can count my supposed slew of one night stands on one hand and still have a finger left. Hell, the same goes for the girls I've had in my bed my entire life.

But I'm not about to admit that to Libby when she could turn into my fake girlfriend. Not when she and every single person who's known me since my freshmen year sees me as the troublemaker of the hockey team.

It's my own fault for the reputation I have. God knows I've stirred up a lot of unnecessary fights. Based on the words Libby just assaulted me with, I've got my work cut out for me if I want any chance of going from instigating playboy to dedicated star player.

"Sure, whatever you say, Lib." Taking off my hat, I nervously run my fingers through my hair before placing it backward again. "But I can't have a girlfriend that sleeps around, even if it is a fake one. I'm not a cheater either. So, you decide if you want to start this charade or continue your . . . extracurricular. The only game I'm interested in playing is on the ice."

She snorts. "And fake dating wouldn't be a game?"

"Cut the shit, Libby. You know what I mean." My agitated voice echoes through the kitchen, louder than I intended. Taking a deep breath to calm myself, an idea forms in my head. I need to give her an ultimatum to make a clear decision. "You have until the Beer Olympics to figure it out. Yes or no, we're fake together." I distraughtly run my fingers through my long hair again. "Maybe isn't an option anymore."

"Okay." Confusion furrows her brow. "I just thought we were on the same page . . ."

"I can find another fake girlfriend. It only happens that I asked you because I covered your ass at the beach. I need to rebrand myself—with or without you. I was doing you a favor."

"You're right, you're right." She lets out a heavy sigh. "You're a good friend. I need to be one too." Her brown eyes gleam with apology when they meet mine. "I'll let you know at the Beer Olympics, okay?" She asks in a hushed, gentle tone.

"Sure, Lib." I avert my gaze, looking anywhere but her, unease filling my gut. I need to stop being seen as a womanizer. I could just declare I am taking a vow of celibacy like a monk or a priest, but no one would take me seriously. My "attitude change" is already not being taken seriously so having a fake girlfriend is my best option. But maybe it's more stress than it's worth.

Lucas made me an alternate captain. I need to prove to him I'm turning my act around. No more fights. No more pretending to take girls home. I don't just need him and the rest of the team to start seeing me in a different light, I need to show them who I can be, even if the most anyone will accept is a decent guy. I'll take what I can get.

Libby's now causal tone breaks my spiraling thoughts. "I'm going to head out."

"Do you want me to walk you?" I ask, genuinely wanting to ensure she gets home safely.

"No, that's okay. Syd is leaving too. We'll walk back together." Before sauntering off, she turns to me. "You're not all bad, Blaine Mitchell," she whispers in that same hushed, gentle tone, pressing a soft kiss to my cheek before going to find Sydney.

A single shred of hope takes root in my heart at her words. I hope she means them, and that everyone else will believe them.

I take a swig of my now lukewarm beer. Libby sheepishly waves goodbye as she walks through the house leaving arm and arm with Sydney.

I lace my hands together behind my head, placing them on the brim of my black Wyverns hat. An exasperated breath escapes me.

"Trouble in paradise?" A voice that I can't quite place whispers in my ear, causing me to jump.

"Seems like I'm always scaring you, aren't I, B?" The alluring voice teases me.

Only one person in my life has ever called me "B." Turning, I find the most unexpected girl before me.

"Renee." My lips purse, puzzled. "What are you doing here?" My words come out harsher than I intend. I met the blonde seductress almost three years ago while I was visiting the Wyverns. I haven't seen or talked to her since.

"Is that how you greet all your old friends?" She takes a step toward me again. Instinctively, I take a step back.

"I wouldn't call a one night stand I haven't talked to in almost three years an old friend, Renee," I huff in frustration. Apparently, her lack of response after we spent the night together still hurts my ego.

"Oh, B, don't be bitter. You know you missed me." She closes the gap between us and lightly traces her hand along my cheek, grazing it as if to comfort me but it has the opposite effect.

"Are you going to tell me what you're doing here?" I ask through clenched teeth. "Or are you going to keep playing your little games?"

"You love games, B." She fake pouts again like a spoiled rich girl throwing a tantrum to get her allowance for the week.

"I'm really sick of people pretending like they know me tonight." I walk to the fridge to grab a beer, hoping it will ease the tension filling my gut. Between the unwelcome visit from Renee and Libby giving me shit, I'm ready to call it quits tonight.

"So, was that girl your girlfriend?" Renee pries, taking a step toward me, clearly wanting to eliminate the space I created between us.

Memories from the first time I met Renee three years ago fill me as her question about my love life echoes in my mind. Deja vu.

Taking a long pull of my beer, I finally answer her. "It's none of your concern." My tone is flat, uninterested, and cold. I know all too well that this girl is capable of fucking with my head.

Renee moves closer to me again. "Then I guess that means I can come home with you tonight," she purrs, reaching for my hand.

Instinctively, I turn away. "No, thanks. I'm headed back outside."

My back is to Renee as I start to open the sliding door.

"Wait," she calls out, choked with emotion which stops me in my tracks.

Slowly, I face her and wait for an explanation.

"Blaine, I'm sorry I just." She lets out an exaggerated sigh. "I've missed you."

Once again, the emerald eyed beauty tempts me to play the bad boy part I was casted as right away when I came to West. One more night can't hurt, right? No one would even know.

She reaches for my hand again, this time I allow her to grab it, and she quickly pulls me to the front door to leave. As if following orders, I obediently follow.

"Your place?" she asks, her voice laced with lust and greed.

The single syllable word flies out of my mouth before I can think with my head instead of my cock, "Yes."

"Good boy," she lulls, entrancing me in her intoxicating call of temptation.

Good boy? That is exactly what I need to be.

Chapter Thirty-Two
Blaine

Memories from three years ago stir, playing in my head like a movie.

"Why the long face?" An unfamiliar sultry voice coos, startling me.

"Sorry, I didn't mean to make you jump. I just got here." The bright-eyed, blonde hums. Her radiant face and intense green eyes are as unrecognizable as her siren-like voice.

"No worries," I murmur. "I just didn't know anyone else was inside. The party's out there—in case you missed it."

I've been avoiding going out to the party with the team. A sense of unease sits in my gut. I'm not one of them. Sure, one of the freshmen I was with most of the day while visiting the school invited me, but I don't belong out there. I'm not a Wyvern, not yet anyways.

Whenever my mind thinks of the possibility of finally playing college hockey and escaping my life, peace floods my senses. I really hope to be a Wyvern.

When I graduate next year, I can finally escape my deranged family. That fills me with more joy than I've felt in years. Well, except for when my skates hit the ice and my mind is focused on only one thing—the game.

I swear my mother and her new husband—I guess I really should stop calling him new after eight years, but I refuse to call him my stepfather—will throw money at anything if it means not having to spend actual time with me or my sister. Even though my mother claims they love us all the same, she and her new husband have their own kids now.

Works for me.

I'll take their money.

"But you didn't answer my question?" The alluring voice pulls me back to WMU's campus. She brushes her curly golden locks behind her hair, strutting over to stand opposite of me behind the counter.

"Hmmm?" I genuinely forgot what she asked, getting lost in my own thoughts.

"You don't seem to be having a good time." In one swift movement, she swipes my hat, placing it backward on her head.

"No, I mean," I fumble for words, lost in the striking green eyes that just hat-napped me, "it's not like that. I just don't want to overstay my welcome."

"Don't come to hockey parties often?" she asks, cocking an eyebrow at me.

"No. Can I have my hat back?" I run my fingers through my disheveled hair, knowing it won't help much.

"Me either. They suck honestly. Where's your girlfriend?" She inquires as she places the hat forwards on her head, instead of handing it over.

"Doesn't exist," I grumble nervously.

"Lucky me." A sly grin slides across her angelic face. "What's that?" She points at the beer in my hand, clearly knowing alcohol is inside the red solo cup. Willingly passing her my cup, I hope the alcohol distracts her so I can swipe my hat back. I don't care how hot this girl is, she makes my blood boil with irritation.

"Got anything other than beer you can share with me?" She winces, taking a sip.

"If you go join the party, I'm sure there's plenty of whatever you want out back." I lean over the counter and snatch my hat back.

"Hey, that was a cheap shot!" she shouts after taking another drink of my disgustingly lukewarm beer that I've been sipping on for the last hour. "And I don't want to go outside. Hockey parties aren't my thing."

"Two things you should know about me, mystery girl. One, if there's an opportunity, I'll always take the open shot. Two, I don't let anyone take my hat."

"Typical hockey player." She rolls her eyes at me as I readjust my hat back on its rightful place atop my head.

"I don't play for the Wyverns," I correct her, but curiosity takes over me. "If you don't want to go outside to the party, why are you even here?"

"Great question," she mumbles. Sadness and confusion cloud her face for a flicker of a second.

"Keep the beer." I turn to head back outside to reluctantly rejoin the party.

"You're just going to leave me here?" She whines loudly, seeking attention. "That's not very nice."

A hollowness starts to linger in my chest. This stranger saying I'm not nice hits me in a sore spot. College will be a fresh start for me, even if technically I haven't started yet. It's not official I'll come to West, but I don't want anything to ruin my chances of making sure I'm not pegged as the bad boy or asshole like I was in high school.

"Would you care to join me, m'lady?" I extend my hand out to her chivalrously.

With unexpected force, especially from such a petite girl, she takes my hand and pulls me to her, our bodies mere inches apart.

"I wouldn't mind sharing something other than a drink," her whisper tickles my ear and sends blood rushing to my groin.

It's been so long since I had that type of release . . . The season hasn't even started yet and my stress level is consistently rising. With a shake of my head, I try to release the thought. I'm trying to rebuild my reputation.

"Sorry, mystery girl, I'm not that easy." Putting some distance between us, I decide to try to have an actual conversation. "What's your name?"

"I never said you were," She pouts. "I've never seen you before, and you said you're not on the team."

"That's accurate," I respond, deciding not to tell her I'm just visiting campus. If she knew I was just a senior in high school, I doubt she would pay me an ounce of attention. Playing it cool and trying to strike up a conversation again, I tell her my name.

She slowly saunters closer, closing the gap between us, causing heat to rush to my groin. I should back away but no one has turned me on like this in, God, I don't even know how long.

"Don't you want to go to the party?" The words fall out of my mouth almost in a slur, distracted by how close this green-eyed flirt is to me.

"Not really." She shrugs. She brings her lips so close to mine, they almost touch. The warmth of her breath grazes my face. "I would much rather have a party for two."

Her eyes sparkle with mischievous delight as she leans into me, daring me to make the next move, but I stand my ground. This girl likes to play games. I can play along.

"So, B." She emphasizes the nickname she just bestowed upon me. "Do I have to steal your hat again for attention. Or are you going to take me home?"

Each word out of her mouth is like a siren's song, seductive and dangerous.

"Tell me your name." My voice is a low growl demanding instead of asking her name. This girl plays games; I can play too.

"If I tell you my name, are you going to be my prize?" she croons, wildness flickers in her eyes.

My lack of response doesn't sit well with her, she pushes her body against me. Her glimmering green eyes look up to meet mine. They are the color of greed, desire, lust.

As I nod agreeing to her terms, she whispers, "It's Renee." Each word softly vibrates my lips with how close her mouth still is to mine.

"I live two blocks away," I quickly lie. I might not live there but the dorm room I'm staying in while I visit is two blocks away. She seals her mouth against mine, greedily opening my mouth with her tongue. My hat lifts from my head just as she breaks our embrace. She puts it on. Again.

Her body presses firmly on mine, my erection growing as she pushes her hips against me. She leans over and whispers seductively in my ear, "If I give you the hat back, will you wear it while you fuck me?"

Stunned into silence by her promiscuous ask, I don't respond.

A mischievous grin spreads across Renee's face as she gives me back my cap and yanks me to the front door to leave.

Frantically taking off my sock, I put it on the door handle and locking the dorm room door.

Renee giggles. "I didn't know people actually did that. I thought it was just in movies."

Hell, if I know. I'm not even in college yet. My shoulders shrug in response to her.

Renee takes a slight step back from me. "You don't think anyone will come in, right?" Her eyes are wide with what looks like fear. "We can't get caught," she mutters under her breath.

"Would be the first time someone ignored that signal." Confidence fills me as I nod toward the door acting like I belong on this campus and have girls in my fake dorm room frequently.

Dragging a chair from the desk in the corner, I place it in front of the door to reassure her. Then, double check it's locked—despite knowing I locked it seconds ago.

"Oh." A devious smirk slides across her face. "You use that signal often?"

Shrugging in response again, I discard my shirt in the corner of the room, making sure to put my hat right back on.

"Well, B." Her hands move seductively across my chest, sending shivers of desire to every nerve ending in my body. Her lips find mine, kissing me as if she needs me to breathe. Her hands push against my chest, guiding me toward the back of the room. With a gentle shove, she pushes me onto the bed while taking her dress off in one swift, seductive motion, "Those girls aren't me."

Just like when I first met her, Renee sucked me back into her web like a venomous spider capturing her prey tonight. But it'll never happen again. I used her, just like she used me. Nothing more, nothing less.

Now, I need to focus on hockey and being the best fake boyfriend Libby could ever want. Every fiber of my being needs her to say yes to being my fake girlfriend at the Beer Olympics.

I can't be lured by Renee's siren song again.

Chapter Thirty-Three

Lucas

My finger press *snooze* for the third time in a row on my phone alarm. One more drink at the party and my head would be spinning from nursing a gnarly hangover. My eyes long to be closed and exhaustion riddles my body. Good thing practice isn't for a few hours.

Ensuring a hangover doesn't creep up on me, I eat a greasy but semi-healthy breakfast before taking the longest cold shower of my life. Drinking and partying have never been my forte, I've always been dedicated to hockey, but it comes with the territory.

My eyes were playing tricks on me last night, I swear I saw my ex-girlfriend. It must've been a combination of drinking more than I usually do and hearing her name for the first time in years, despite it technically being someone else's name.

The cool droplets graze my skin, instantly making me feel revived as if they molded to me forming a whole new person. The water relieves me, easing the thoughts of my ex from my mind and clearing my head for the day ahead.

After throwing on some sweats, I settle into my desk, ready to start looking at some of my old notes on players and other hockey teams. My heart plummets like a stone seeing the new pocket book I started last year is in the desk drawer, but Nick Bellinger's player notebook that Laur let me borrow is nowhere in sight. The calmness the shower brought me disappears completely.

My room looks like a tornado came through, I ravaged it from top to bottom, but the notebook still hasn't shown up.

Glancing at the clock, my pulse quickens with only forty-five minutes until practice starts. My anxiety rockets sky high, I really need time to meditate before I'm on the ice or I'll play like shit. Nick's notebook search will have to continue when I get back.

My heart rate doesn't slow while I power walk to the arena. My chest tightens as I enter the locker room. Each breath becomes harder to take. Without thinking, I practically collapse down on the floor in front of my cubby and open my meditation app, not bothering to put headphones in. My eyelids instinctively close and I let the tranquil tunes and gentle, soft voice surround me, taking over as I take deep breath after deep breath.

In.

Out.

In.

Out.

The two words are on repeat in my head trying to bring calmness over me and soothe my breathing. After a minute, my heart thumps at an almost normal speed, no longer racing. Giving myself over to the healing sounds, I focus on each breath leaving and entering my body.

My eyes snap open at the noise of footsteps.

"Shit, I tried to be as quiet as a mouse I swear." Blaine's eyes fall to me on the ground.

My face heats and my eyes quickly dart away from his. I scramble to pause the music. The only sound I can hear is my heartbeat picking up speed again.

"I really should do that more," Blaine mutters, taking a seat on the ground across from me. He clears his throat. "When my parents were getting divorced, my mom forced me into therapy."

Running my hand threw my hair, I stay silent. Embarrassed that Blaine's witnessing me meditating.

"The ice was the only place I felt at peace until I had a panic attack," he continues, ignoring my lack of response. "That anxiety rushing in and taking over my body made me feel like I was dying."

"Really?" I'm not sure I've had a full-on panic attack, but I don't want to experience one.

"Honestly, it was scary." Blaine casts a wary glance around the room, avoiding looking at me. "Talking to my therapist about it was the only time I felt like I got anything out of therapy. He taught me how to meditate like that."

Letting out a quiet chuckle, I reply, "I don't think I'm very good at it."

"No one's good at it," Blaine assures me. "It's fucking hard not to focus on yourself when the world around you doesn't stop."

Letting out a sigh, I confess, "It doesn't always work for me."

"It didn't always work for me either." Blaine lets out a deep sigh. "But I haven't had a panic attack since my sophomore year of high school, so it had to have helped."

An awkward silence settles between us.

"You know," Blaine's voice is quiet. "A lot of famous hockey players meditate."

"Really?"

"Yeah." Blaine starts to casually list a few, "Zach Hyman from the Leafs, Colin Wilson that played for the Avs, that goalie from Buffalo . . . I can't remember his name but I remember he did an NHL interview about it."

Blaine's unfazed that I meditate. He's even supporting me. Each player he lists off brings me a sense of relief that washes over me like a warm breeze on a hot summer day. I'm not alone in this.

Blaine snaps his fingers in the air. "Even your boy Toews from Chicago did a five-week meditation and yoga retreat or something like that when he took that time off the ice."

The locker room door squeaks open bringing echoing footsteps and chatter in with it.

"Thanks for all that," I whisper to Blaine. He offers me a hand, pulling me up off the ground.

With a pat on my shoulders, his understanding gaze meets my wide flustered eyes. "Anytime, Luc."

Never in my life would I think that Blaine Mitchell would be the one to relate to me about meditating and anxiety.

Practice starts per usual with drills. Energy courses through me, I fly on my skates finishing every single drill in record time. I've got wheels today, feeling unstoppable.

Tapping my stick impatiently on the ice, I'm buzzing to get through drills and into scrimmaging. Joy flickers, then flashing into a full-blown smile thinking about Coach Andres' new lines with Ryder, Blaine, and me on offense. There's a new fire lit inside me today and I am ready to dominate.

A whistle fills the arena. Coach signals for us to all regroup around the bench. My eyes fall to Laur with a high ponytail and eager grin. Excitement lights up her face, she's radiant.

Laur opens her mouth, but a familiar voice reaches my ears that is not hers. A voice I haven't heard in years.

"Hi, Luc."

My eyes widen in disbelief as they collide with the evasive green eyes of my ex-girlfriend. My chest grows heavy as if my heart is in shackles.

"Raven?" The name is a toxic whisper on my tongue. My heart beat drums with panic, vibrating the shackles with each thump as my brows crease with confusion. What the hell is she doing here?

"Please help me welcome the new PR members," Laur interrupts. Her gaze meets mine, her eyes cloudy with uncertainty and hints of fear.

Laur continues introducing each new member. She starts to explain some of the new ideas and events they have for this year.

The guys make snide comments around me at the picnic basket auction, but I haven't heard a single word Laur's said. The chains around my chest tighten with each breath I take.

In.

Out.

Raven is here.

My ex-girlfriend is here.

In.

Out.

The fire inside me turns into raging flames of chaos. There's no hope in calming it, but I keep trying to avoid letting it consume me.

In.

Out.

In.

Holy shit.

Out.

Laur's team starts to turn around, I scramble as close as possible to the boards and grab her arm, yanking her back.

Through clenched teeth, I whisper, "Lauren, how the hell is my ex-girlfriend part of your PR and marketing team? And why the hell is she?"

Her blue eyes are as wide as saucers, frenzy flickering in them. She hastily scans the arena around us, making sure to keep her voice low so no one can hear.

"What the hell are you talking about?" Her tone is low and laced with alarm.

A deep breath fills my lungs but does nothing to ease my hysteria. "That girl," I hiss quietly, "is my ex-girlfriend, Raven."

"I thought . . ." she trails off, a distant look in her gaze.

"It's her." I confirm, my voice shaking and on edge. I run my hands down my face. My nerves are now lit up like a live wire.

"How . . ." Laur's voice is barely audible. "I'll get to the bottom of it."

Laur plants a tender kiss on unmoving lips. Her distress mirrors mine. She nervously twirls her hair around her finger.

"I'm sorry," she whispers. "I swear I didn't know."

"I know," I lean in to kiss her cheek. This isn't her fault. "I trust you. I know it's not your fault."

"I'll get to the bottom of it," she vows again with more certainty. "I promise."

As I watch her leave, the weight on my heart lifts a fraction just knowing how much I love her. It will be harder on her to have Raven here than it will on me, but I am still so caught off guard.

What the hell kind of game is Raven playing now?

Chapter Thirty-Four
Laur

Each breath I take causes pain through my entire body as if I am breathing polluted air. How is Raven Matthews the same Raven Lucas dated? She must have changed her last name.

Thinking about how I'll have to spend an entire year working with her and watching her with him feels like a punch to the gut. Jealousy flares my nostrils.

"Lauren."

Turning around, my eyes fall to the conniving girl. Raven's gaze is full of remorse but the only thing I can see in the dark green of her eyes is a snake in the grass. A muscle ticks in my jaw as if I'm ready to chew her head off.

"Can I talk to you?" Raven asks in a hushed tone. "I want to explain."

It takes every ounce of self-control I have to hold it together and not scream in her face.

"I . . ." Restraint coils tight beneath my skin as each word comes out hasty but collected and smooth. "I've got to go."

As soon as I'm out the front doors, my feet launch me into a dead run toward home. The world blurs around me as tears pool in my eyes.

The slam of the front door echoes throughout the house as I force it closed behind me, falling to the floor against it. Yanking out my phone, I dial Bren's number.

No answer.

My fingers quickly tap her name, calling her again.

"C'mon, pick up," I mutter as the ringing continues.

She doesn't answer. Logic tells me she's probably working but my brain is operating on emotion, not logic. Putting my head in my hands, I let out a frantic cry and let the tears fall.

The tears don't stop. They cover my cheeks, my shirt, some even manage to find their way to the hardwood floor. Sniffling, I try Bren one more time.

"Please pick up," I desperately sob.

Still no answer.

My phone's in the air, thrown out of frustration without a second thought. With a loud *thud*, it lands on the living room carpet.

"Shit!" I wail. The last thing I need today is a broken phone on top of everything else.

The front door hits me in the back.

"Laur?" Libby's voice calls, trying to open the door and hitting me again.

"One second," I blubber, dragging myself a few feet forward on the floor.

"Can I come in now?" Libby inquires softly through the crack in the door.

"Okay," I respond, choking back tears.

The second Libby lays eyes on me, puffy-eyed and distraught in our entry way, she bends down beside me. "Laur, what's wrong?"

My answer gets lost as I break down in tears. Libby tries to calm me, rubbing my back in a soothing motion and telling me everything will be okay. I pray she's right.

Slowly, I move from sprawled on the floor to sitting, resting my head on Libby's shoulder. The tears still stream down my face.

"Do you want to talk about it?" Libby asks quietly.

"I need a tissue," I snivel.

Libby immediately stands, going to the bathroom and grabbing me the entire box of issues.

"Thanks," I mumble, blowing my nose so hard it hurts.

My phone rings and Bren's name comes across the screen, but I need a minute to gather myself.

"Will you still be free in fifteen minutes?" I bawl into the phone, my voice hoarse and distraught.

"What's wrong, Laur?" Bren's bubbly voice, a gentle whisper.

"Will you still be free in fifteen minutes?" I ask again with a sniffle.

"Yeah," Bren starts, but before she can say another word, I tell her I'll call her back.

Every muscle in my body aches as I get up off the ground. Handing Libby back the box of tissues, I tell her I'm going to take a shower, then will fill her and Bren in at the same time. I need time to process this before I talk.

My tears mix with the warm water as it runs down my body. Question after question plagues my mind.

Why is she here?

Did she know who I was?

Is she still in love with him?

Will she try to win him back?

My heart breaks wrapping my mind around the last question. Even if she does want him back, Lucas loves me. The little he shared about Raven wasn't positive, I doubt he would be interested even if I wasn't in the picture, which brings me back to the first question again.

"What the hell is she doing here?" I whisper to the shower walls, wishing they would give me the answers, so I don't have to talk to her to find out.

With sopping wet hair, I pull on my comfiest sweatshirt that technically belongs to Lucas and head down the stairs. Each step makes me more mopey.

"She's out of the shower," Libby says into her phone. "Here, sweetie." She hands me a cup of piping hot liquid. "I made you some tea."

Taking the mug from her, I instantly place it on the counter. "Thanks, but it's at least ninety degrees outside."

"I told you, Bren," Libby hisses into the phone. "It's too hot for tea! I knew she wouldn't want it."

"Yeah, yeah, whatever," Libby responds to whatever Bren said. "You're going on speaker."

My stomach churns, and I reach for the tea. "I'm going to need to sit for this," I mutter into the cup as I take a sip and burn my entire mouth.

Cozying up into the corner of the couch, I pull a blanket over me despite my earlier comment on the heat. I need all the comfort I can get.

"Raven Matthews," my voice cracks on her name, "is Lucas' ex girlfriend."

"What the fuck?" Libby spits each word out.

"What did she say?" Bren chimes in from the speaker phone. "I can't hear."

"Oh sorry," Libby walks over to me, handing me the phone. "Raven Matthews is Lucas' ex-girlfriend." Libby speaks into the phone. "She's a new girl we brought on to the team." She hands me back the phone and whispers, "All yours now."

"Wait?" Bren's muffled voice comes from the speaker phone. "But how is that even possible?"

My heart sinks in my stomach as if it's made of pure lead. "I don't know," I whisper.

"Her last name isn't Matthews though, it's Harriet or Hettington, or something with an H," Bren clarifies.

"Lucas asked me why his ex is now on the PR team"—tears sting my eyes—"It's definitely her."

"She must have changed it," Bren mutters.

Taking a sip of my tea, I can't help but wonder what would make a nineteen year old girl change her last name.

"Wait." Libby's jaw drops. "Was it Harrington?"

"Yes!" Bren shouts, her voice almost bubbly.

"Holy shit," Libby whispers.

A crease forms between my brows as confusion sets in. How did Libby know her previous last name?

"I only met her once," Bren rushes to fill the silence. "I should have helped with interviews. I would have recognized her."

"Holy shit," Libby squeals with excitement.

"What's happening? Why is she excited?" Bren questions frantically. "Aren't we upset?"

"Yes, we are upset," Libby confirms, her eyes full of sympathy, "but do you know who her freaking mom is?"

"Clearly, I didn't know who the hell she was," I mutter, annoyance filling me.

"I would bet money that her mom is Holly Harrington." Libby's eyes are as wide as saucers. "It all makes sense now."

"Don't worry, Bren, " I speak directly into the phone. "I'm just as confused as you are."

"As in H. Harrington?" Bren slowly replies.

"Yes!" Libby shrieks with excitement. "As in H. Harrington, the fashion designer."

The pieces of the puzzle click into place. Her experience in the fashion industry at such a young age. Her mention of family ties to the industry. Grabbing my phone from my hoodie pocket, I type in H. Harrington.

Holy shit is right.

There are millions of articles about the cutting edge designer. Over one million followers on social media. A brand website. Clicking on the image tab, I quickly see the resemblance.

"But that doesn't explain anything," I think out loud, "about what the hell she is doing here."

"I know, babe," Bren breathes loudly into the phone. "There's only one person who has those answers for you."

The room falls silent. I know I have to talk to Raven, but I have zero desire to be in the same room as the girl let alone have a conversation.

"You can do hard things, Laur," Bren's static-riddled voice breaks the silence. "I'm sorry you have to deal with this. I love you and I'm here for you."

"Thank you, love you too, Brennie Bean." I let out an exhausted sigh. "I'll text or call you later this week."

"You better," Bren demands. "I want an update on all this drama."

"I will." Hitting the end call button, the room goes quiet again and stillness settles in.

"Do you want to talk more about it?" Libby asks as she grabs her phone.

Shaking my head, I stare into my tea. "I think I just want to be alone for a little while."

"If you need me, I'm here," Libby reassures me, "whether you need me to help you get information, need a shoulder to cry on, or someone to punch her in the face. I'm here."

"No," I spit out quickly. "No more fighting."

"Yeah, you're right," Libby jokes with a giggle. "Tyler has done enough recently. I'll wait at least a week."

A small chuckle flutters out of me. "Terrible joke."

"Great joke," Libby argues. "But Lucas worships the ground you walk on, Laur. You have nothing to worry about there."

"I know," I reply. And I do. I'm not worried about Lucas wanting her but that doesn't mean I want to spend almost every day with his ex-girlfriend.

Libby shuffles upstairs and to her room, leaving me alone with my thoughts. Lucas told me last year that they broke up because she hated how much he put hockey first. Her joining the program to support the Wyverns makes no sense.

There's a lot to uncover but I'm determined to know every single detail of why Raven Matthews, or I guess Raven Harrington, is here.

Chapter Thirty-Five
Lucas

Seeing my ex-girlfriend at the start of my hockey practice with my current girlfriend feels like a fever dream. Why is she here and why did she join the PR and marketing team to support MY freaking hockey team? She has to be playing games.

I know the dream is a reality as soon as she comes into the arena again. Her green eyes lock with mine the second I open the door, but I instantly look away as disbelief and frustration fill me.

Blowing off steam on the ice after practice was supposed to take my mind off this bizarre situation, not put me smack dab in the middle of it.

"Luc, I'm sorry—" Raven starts. I instantly cut her off.

"Honestly, I don't give a fuck Raven," I snap at her. Those eyes I used to see my future in turn a deep emerald, sorrow painted on her face.

Each stomp of my foot is louder than the one before as I storm off, hoping she'll leave.

"I . . ." She starts again, her voice cracking on the single word as she trails behind me

My racing heartbeat pulses in my ears. This girl means nothing to me anymore, but that doesn't mean I want her around.

I spin on my heels, facing her. Before she can continue, the words spill out of me like a leaky faucet.

"I'm serious, Raven. I don't care." My lungs fill with a deep, calming breath, trying to keep my head level and not let the rage from how she hurt me take over. "I don't know what you're doing here, but don't make Laur regret giving you a spot on her team. If I were her, I would've already kicked you off of it."

Her emerald eyes find mine empty ones. I stare deep into them, not breaking eye contact. She knows that I mean every word that comes next. "I'm happier than I've ever been. I already have a lot of stress going on in my life. I don't need you to add to it because of some petty shit."

Raven turns her face, trying to hide the tears that fill her eyes. I should feel remorse, but I don't.

"Luc, I promise I am not here to win you back." She wipes a stray tear from her cheek. "I have no intention—"

"Good," I interrupt, again. I do mean it. I'm happier than I have ever been. Laur's the one for me. My heart knew she was the instant our eyes met, but seeing Raven again has solidified that for me. Raven was just a gateway love. Laur is the love of my life.

Pivoting toward the locker room, Raven calls to me. "Wait." I turn back to face her, waiting for her to say whatever it is she needs to get off her chest.

"I really am sorry, Lucas," she whispers.

"Why are you even here, Raven?" I might believe she's sorry, but there is no possible way it's a coincidence she's at my school, now supporting my team. "Why did you even apply in the first place? You have no interest in hockey, aside from the players," I know I shouldn't make the comment but it rolls off my tongue so easily, I couldn't help it. Even if I've moved on, being cheated on, especially when it involves one of my teammates, is still shitty. No one deserves that. And because of Raven and her antics, I hated Blaine and painted him as an asshole instantly.

Raven rolls her eyes at my dig. "So you do care."

"No," I assure her. "I don't." Mercy does fill me. In fact, the opposite seems to flow through me as my jaw tightens with frustration. "It just sucks that you had cheated on me with one of my fucking players. If you're gonna be unfaithful, there's so many other people you could've picked."

She takes a step toward me, and as if on a reflex I take a step back, not wanting her to be close to me. I have no desire to be anything to her, not even a friend.

She scrunches her face as if she's just been hit in the gut and whispers, "It wasn't intentional. I just need attention."

"Not surprising. You always did." I sigh when I make the realization. "We weren't good for each other. Even well before you went and did that."

"I know," she cries. Tears cover her cheeks. "I was just a kid. I'm sorry. I came here because I want to learn and grow. As a person and more."

"Sure." I just want to leave this conversation and go home to see my actual girlfriend instead of being at the rink now. My kind, sweet, supportive girlfriend, who would never cheat on me.

"I mean it. I'm tired of living in my mother's shadow." Her tears still flow silently down her face. "I need to learn something different than fashion. I need to disassociate myself with her and her name." She sniffles, trying to keep herself together.

My eyebrows raise with curiosity. I knew her mom was unkind and hard on her. But she's one of the most famous fashion designers now, I'm surprised she doesn't want to be associated with her. But frankly, I don't care enough to ask.

"I don't want her to be the reason I find success." Raven wipes at her eyes and tries to steady her shaky voice. "She claims she's the only reason I've gotten anywhere with my reporting career. I want to pave my own path."

Raven takes a deep sigh as she leans against the wall. "I don't need or want anyone. I can do it all on my own, and I need to prove it to her. That's why I came here."

Silence fills the space between us, her sobs now quiet.

"I swear I applied to other programs and other schools, but you know how great this one is," she mutters.

Sadly, I do know. It's one of the best college programs in the country, if not the best for hockey PR.

"Look at me," I command. Her watery eyes meet my harsh stare. "You do anything to her, and I promise you that you will regret ever stepping on this campus. Do you understand me?"

Her eyes go hollow as her mouth drops.

"Who even are you, Lucas?" Raven asks her voice low.

"Someone who will protect the woman I love at all costs. Tell me you understand me, Raven."

"I understand. I'm happy for you. I really am." She nods, trying to assure me. "I'm not here to cause any issues. I'll prove it to you." She pauses, swallowing loudly before saying, "And I'll stay away from Blaine Mitchell."

My fist clench in frustration. *Who does she think she is?*

"Let's get one thing straight," I growl. There's no hint of sympathy in any bone in my body. "I don't give a fuck what or who you do. As long as you're not interfering with my life or Laur's or the hockey team's success this year—I couldn't care less."

Her shoulders shutter as her sobs fill the arena once again

"But don't fucking break him," the words are out of my mouth before I can stop myself. "You dig your nails in deep and you don't let go. He has a lot of potential. He doesn't deserve for you to fuck with his head or be treated like you treat people. No one does."

"I'm not the same person," she mumbles with a trembling voice.

"I'll believe it when I see it. As far as I'm concerned and as far as I can see, you still are."

My heavy, angry steps drown out her cries as I stomp off to the locker room. I've had enough of her, but I know she isn't going anywhere.

Between impressing scouts, the pressure as Captain, and now my Raven being here—the stress of this season might end me.

Chapter Thirty-Six
Blaine

*F*uck.

Her name isn't Renee. Just like I did that first night we met, she deceived me with lies to get me in bed with her.

It all makes sense. The fear in her eyes when she asked if someone would come in three years ago. How she never texted me back. The fact I haven't seen her in almost three years.

The rest of practice is a blur.

"Mitch, c'mon!" Someone yells at me for missing another pass. I just got announced as one of the alternate captains; I need to get my head in the fucking game.

Somehow, I manage to make it through the rest of practice without losing my shit, but the second I'm in the locker room, I grab my phone to ask Libby for details.

Me: Who is that girl?

Me: Libby? Who is she?

Libby: Her name is Raven

Me: But who is she?

Me: Why are Laur and Lucas on edge?

Libby: Don't tell anyone, okay?

Me: You know I won't.

Me: You can trust me.

Libby: She's Lucas' ex-girlfriend.

Libby: They dated all of high school until his freshman year of college.

Libby: No idea why she is here.

Libby: Shit's about to get messy.

Panic consumes me and nausea fills my gut, surging through me like I'm seasick.

Fuck.

Not only did I sleep with Lucas' ex-girlfriend days ago while I'm trying to turn a new leaf and stop being the infamous bad boy of the hockey team, but I hooked up with her three years ago when she was still his girlfriend.

There's no way he can know. Right?

Acknowledgements

The continuation of Lucas and Laur's story wouldn't be possible without YOU, dear reader. Thank you for making my debut novel, *One Shot,* bigger than I could ever imagine. Because of you, *Summer Shot* and *Best Shot* (Wyverns Book Three) became more than just an idea. They became a dream come freaking true. All because of you picked up my book.

To my wonderful bestie and assistant Miranda — thank you for keeping me grounded, open minded, encouraged, and making me laugh so hard I cry. This journey truly wouldn't be as rewarding and fulfilling without you by my side.

Thank you to my amazing Beta readers – Ashley, Kaitlyn, Keri and Miranda. I appreciate you reading (my very rough) drafts, providing your feedback, and always cheering me on. You each have truly become true friends. I am so grateful for you all.

This book also wouldn't be possible without my street team. If I'm being honest. . . I'm still in awe I have a freaking street team, y'all make me feel like such a bad ass! I am endlessly thankful for every single one of you. Your support means so much. Thank you for believing in me.

Cayla, my incredible editor. You truly are doing the Lord's work dealing with my lack of grammar skills. I am so grateful to have your guidance, recommendations, and friendship. I thought you should know that I will never think of "MW" as Merriam-Webster and I'm not sorry about it (I hope you get that lyric pun!)

Thank you, Tina, my incredible artist, for somehow always pulling the vision from my head and making it come to life in the most beautiful way. Your talent will never cease to amaze me.

To my sweet friend Kara— thank you for being such an amazing mentor. Your encouragement, advice, and friendship mean the world.

Thank you to my family and close friend for always rooting for me and my big dreams, even if it means I'm busier than I've ever been. You're make the big dreams worth sharing.

Lastly, mom and dad— thank you for having such an inspiring love story, for always supporting me, and always telling me that I can accomplish anything I set my mind to.

Lucas and Laur aren't quite done yet – *Best Shot* is just around the corner.

About The Author

A.C. Wonderland has always loved telling stories for as long as she can remember. When she was eight, she wrote and drew an entire twenty-page book for school... even though the assignment was to write one page.

The reality is life isn't always easy. Sometimes you need an escape from everyday life. A.C. thrives on writing novels that let a reader get lost in a whirlwind romance.

A.C never thought she would be an author. But, in July 2024, her first book came pouring out of her. She created a thirty six chapter outline and wrote the first three chapters of *One Shot*, her debut novel, in less than two hours. It was evident that she had a story that was begging to be shared.

You only have one life to live—A.C is taking her "one shot" to pursue her dreams of becoming an author.

When she's not writing, A.C. loves traveling the country, frequenting country music concerts, and, of course, going to hockey games. She lives in Nashville with her dog, Guinness, but is originally from the suburbs of Chicago.

Catch her on Instagram or TikTok at @acwonderlandwrites or check out her website www.acwonderlandwrites.com.

See what she's reading - www.goodreads.com/acwonderland.

www.ingramcontent.com/pod-product-compliance
Lightning Source LLC
Chambersburg PA
CBHW071109100726
47908CB00008B/2317

9798991979238